I0726196

THE AWAKENING

BOOK 1 OF THE BLOODMOON WARS (A PARANORMAL SHIFTER SERIES PREQUEL TO LUNA RISING)

SARA SNOW

This is a work of fiction. Names, characters, places, and incidents either are products of the author's imagination or are used fictitiously. Any similarity to actual events or locales or persons, living or dead, is entirely coincidental.

© 2021 Sara Snow

No part of this publication may be reproduced, stored in or introduced into a retrieval system, or transmitted in any form or by any means (electronic, mechanical, photocopying, recording, or otherwise) without the prior written permission of the copyright owner. The author acknowledges the trademarked status and trademark owners of various products referenced in this work of fiction, which have been used without permission. The publication/use of the trademarks is not authorized, associated with, or sponsored by the trademark owners.

1

———

ELINOR

Rain clouds gathered overhead, and thunder rumbled in the distance as the sun began to set. The beautiful splash of orange and red signifying sunset was nowhere in sight. So, like everyone else, I hurried to get the last items I needed from the market before heading home.

With the hood of my cloak down, a sudden heavy wind had my hair dancing wildly around me, blinding me momentarily. I swatted the strands away from my face. "Um, yes, sorry, I'll take three," I said to the woman behind the stall.

She held out bags of seasoning.

"I'll have those onions as well," I added.

"Hey, are you done?" my best friend Skye asked anxiously. "I really hate the rain."

As I hastily tossed the onions into my bag, I glanced over my shoulder to see her frowning deeply. "Yeah," I told her as I walked away. "I'm almost done. I just need . . ." My words trailed off as I looked around the market, trying to find a vendor who had what I was looking for. "Oh, there, rabbits. Hey, Mr. Wilber!"

A frail human looked up from where he was stuffing a dead rabbit into a crate. "Elinor, how are you?"

"I'm good, just doing a bit of shopping for Mother." I stepped up to his stall.

He removed the rabbit from the crate. "I think this one will do, yes?" the old man inquired. "A gift for your sweet mother."

I smiled as he held it out to me but shook my head wildly. "Thanks, Mr. Wilber, but I can't take this for free."

He waved his hand dismissively. "Nonsense—it's a fine rabbit."

"Oh, I agree, which is why I have to—"

Skye stretched her hand out towards Mr. Wilber. "Oh, you know how this one is, Mr. Wilber. I'll take it for her. You go on and pack up now. Get home before this rain starts." She grabbed my arm, pulling me away while smiling and waving goodbye with the rabbit in her other hand. She turned to look at me. "I was not about to stand there and listen to you two go back and forth." She shoved the rabbit at me. "Take it, and let's go."

"Goddess, you're bossy sometimes," I teased with a chuckle.

A clap of thunder echoed above us.

I looked up at the darkening sky and wondered if I'd make it home before the rain started. I'd hoped to secretly practice a few new fighting techniques I'd picked up until sunset, but my mother interrupted my carefully laid plans. Now here I was, stuck with shopping, even though she could have asked someone else.

Skye whimpered beside me, hugging herself under her

brown cloak, her dark brown doe eyes darting from side to side with anxiety.

Ever since we were kids, she'd always hated the rain. But it had gotten worse after her first transformation. She'd shifted into her wolf form for the first time during a thunderstorm, and it hadn't been a smooth transformation. It had taken her three painful hours to shift entirely, so it was never far from her mind. Now, whenever we had a bad thunderstorm, she became anxious and occasionally, even a little mean.

"I'm sorry I kept you out for so long. I shouldn't have asked you to join me."

She shrugged. "I wanted to come, and we didn't know it would rain. I got a day off from work. Why didn't someone tell me that becoming a pack doctor was this time-consuming?"

I laughed as we made our way through the crowd. "That's what you get for trying to avoid joining the Werewolf Guard."

She growled in the back of her throat. "Not everyone wants to put their lives at risk like you do, Elinor. I'd rather spend my time saving lives versus taking lives."

"The Guards save lives, too," I mumbled to myself as I spotted two guards conversing a few steps in front of us.

As I approached them, they looked our way, and as customary for greeting someone considered a royal, they made fists with their right hands and placed them above their hearts. "Elinor," they greeted me in unison as I walked by. "Do you need us to accompany you home?"

I shook my head. "No, no, we're fine."

Yes, I was a royal, an Alpha-born. I was the first child of

Alpha Grayson, leader of the Blackmoon Pack. While many people might wish they were Alpha-born, my pedigree felt like a curse to me.

I glanced behind me. Both guards were already gone, no doubt off to do what they did best—protecting humans and other supernaturals. That's what the Werewolf Guard was for. Because of our strength and speed, werewolves were the protectors of this world. We were hired by all species to be guardians.

While the world slept, werewolves patrolled the night, hunting those who sought to create havoc. Becoming a member of the Werewolf Guard was my only goal in life.

You might be wondering why I'd want to be a Guard when I was already the firstborn of an Alpha and next in line to lead. Well, if no one has told you, allow me to be the bearer of bad news—a female can never become an Alpha.

Yup, it was wrong, but it was how things have been done since the dawn of time . . . or at least, according to our leaders - the Werewolf Council.

When a female was firstborn, a different role was given to her—the role of a Luna, a mother to more Alphas. As honorable as that was, it wasn't what I wanted. I didn't want to be remembered for my kids. I wanted a reputation as a warrior. That side of me—the part of me that wanted to spend my days training, sweating, and feeling my muscles ache—was something I had to keep to myself, downplaying my true nature every day to act like the daughter my parents wanted.

I'd been born with the strength of an Alpha, but I had to hold back in order to avoid outshining the *true* Alphas, the males in our society who possess all the power.

At a young age, I decided that if I couldn't be an Alpha, I'd become a Guard. At least that way I'd still be protecting my people. But that dream had been shot down by my father. My younger brother, Jackson, would take up the leader's mantle as Alpha someday. But since he was only seven, he still had a long way to go.

"Thief! Stop him!"

I skidded to a halt and spun on my heels as those words met my ears. I spotted a human vendor waving his hand over his head in distress as a shaggy man ran off with his crate of fruit. I narrowed my eyes, realizing the hairy thief was a satyr—a half-goat, half-man supernatural.

My legs moved before I gave them the command as I dropped the bag and the rabbit. I heard Skye's protest, but I only had eyes for my target. I sprinted past the vendor who was still yelling and gesturing furiously.

Despite having a goat-like torso, the thief was surprisingly fast. Satyrs weren't known for their speed, but then, this one wasn't as tall as most of them.

People jumped to the side to avoid being trampled by him as he ran. His light brown dreads blew out behind him as fruit fell out of the crate in his hand. He obviously hadn't thought this through—at the end of this chase, there would be nothing left in that crate.

After a few minutes of running, I growled and removed my cloak, the heavy thing holding me back. I called on my power, and my wolf stirred happily inside me. My eyes turned black, and my fangs elongated. I smiled on the inside as I started gaining on him, the adrenaline pumping within me, urging me onward.

He took a sharp left, dropping the crate in his hand.

I laughed. I could hear Skye running and calling my

name, but I didn't look back as I lunged over a stall to stay on the satyr's heel.

He glanced behind him, and his thick brows rose to his hairline when he saw how close I was.

I grinned at him, flashing my fangs.

Then he took another right, almost colliding with a woman carrying a baby.

With my wolf now enjoying the chase, I fell on all fours and then sprang forward, tackling him. We tumbled on the ground until we came to a stop with me straddling him.

My hand shot out and grabbed his neck, my claws piercing his skin. "I think you dropped your crate, sir."

"Get off me!" he shouted with a slight lisp. Even though he was strong, I had no trouble overpowering him. "I didn't do anything! Get off—" The sound of people gathering around us cut him off.

The owner of the stall he had robbed pushed his way through the crowd. "Thank you so much, Elinor," the proprietor said gratefully.

Unfortunately, some of the excitement I had been feeling faded away as a Werewolf Guard appeared. He gave me a stern look as he picked the satyr up off the ground.

I threw an innocent smile his way. Okay, so I was well-known around these parts for being a thorn in the Guards' sides.

This guard wasn't someone from my pack, but even so, I quickly grabbed Skye's arm and pulled her away. News traveled fast around here. If this got to the ear of a Guard from my pack, my father would hear about it soon after.

"Are you insane?" she sputtered.

I took my cloak from her. "Thanks for picking this up for

me." I threw my cloak on. "If I lose another one, Mother's going to have my head."

She stopped walking, her brows furrowed. "Elinor, can you please take this seriously?"

I stopped walking as well and sighed. With her dark skin, I couldn't tell if she was turning red with rage. But I could read the emotion clearly in her eyes.

A man came up to us as I was about to speak, removing his hood to reveal his face.

When Skye saw who it was, she grinned from ear to ear, her anger at me from the moment before completely forgotten.

I rolled my eyes.

"You know you don't have the right to do the things the Guards do, like apprehending criminals. You could get into trouble," Cyrus—the third person in our best friend trio —chided.

I shrugged. "We've been friends since we were kids, Cyrus. Do you really think I'm ever going to change? I can't just stand by idly when someone needs help." I walked around him. "Plus, I'm an Alpha-born. Remember? I can do what I want."

Ha, if only that were true.

"Oh, please," Skye interjected as we made our way back through the market. "Alpha Grayson is going to be livid if he finds out what you did."

"He's always livid," I mumbled.

They pulled up on either side of me.

I looked at Skye on my left and then at Cyrus on my right.

His black hair was ruffled and curly, a few strands

brushing against his forehead. He narrowed his gray eyes at me and shook his head but smiled nonetheless.

"Where have you been?" I inquired. "You disappeared for a few days. Did you go home?"

He moved his black cloak over his shoulder, revealing a thin cotton shirt rolled up to his elbows and black tribal tattoos on both arms, then shook his head. "No, I haven't been home in a while. I just had a few things to take care of."

Unlike Skye and me, Cyrus was an incubus—a sex demon. And while demons didn't usually mingle with other supernaturals, he was one of my best friends. In fact, he was the only one of his kind to be welcomed into the Blackmoon Pack. As a mere boy, he had proved he wasn't like other demons. Even then, his compassion and kindness had set him apart.

As we walked together, my eyes fell on an old witch walking toward us, her long white hair somewhat tangled and blowing in the wind. Her pale violet eyes openly assessed me, and then her hand rose to point at me. "Be careful, wolf-born. Your blood is special."

The three of us stopped walking and stared at her. I expected her to say something more, an explanation for her comment at the very least, but the old woman simply continued on her way, as if nothing had happened.

Looks of confusion passed between the three of us.

Skye voiced exactly what I was thinking. "What the hell was that?"

I shrugged, but an odd feeling settled within me. "I don't know. Let's get out of here."

Since we could no longer hear the thunder, we assumed it wouldn't rain anymore and took a short detour home.

A five-minute walk through the forest led us to our favorite spot.

I sat down in the thick grass as Skye and Cyrus joined me. "I'm going to ask Father again."

Cyrus groaned, already knowing what I was referring to. "He's going to say no. You know that."

"It can't hurt to try," I countered stubbornly.

He only shook his head. Placing a hand behind his head, he leaned back to lay on the grass.

Skye pushed a strand of curly black hair away from her face. "What are you two talking about?"

"I'm going to ask Father once more if I can join the Werewolf Guard," I told her.

She just stared at me for a moment before breaking out into a fit of laughter. Her chuckles continued until she realized that neither Cyrus nor I were even smiling. Her face fell. "You can't be serious! How many times have you already asked him?" She turned to face me. "I wish he would say yes, I truly do. Because I know it's what you want more than anything. But he'll never agree." She sighed. "Please don't do this again. Just focus on another career path, Elinor. There's so much you can still do without being a Guard. The last time you spoke to your father about this, you guys had a horrible fight."

I reached out and picked a wildflower from the earth. "We always fight."

We sat in silence for a moment as I plucked the petals from the flower, one by one. *He'd say yes, he'd say no. . . .* The relationship between my father and me was a strained one. Other than the fact that I wasn't the boy he had hoped for, I was apparently also too ambitious as well.

"I won't do it," I said firmly as I looked up from the broken flower in my hand. "I won't be carried around from pack to pack like a merchant's goods. When it comes right down to it, I refuse to become a powerless Luna. It's ridiculous how a male Alpha-born inherits power from birth, but a female Alpha-born just automatically becomes a wife for another Alpha. I'm just as strong as many of the men in my pack. I accept that I can't be Alpha, but why can't I join the Guard? Why?"

"We don't question the fact that you're strong, Elinor, but this is a futile battle you're waging with your father—futile for you," Cyrus pointed out.

I knew he was right, but I refused to give up.

Silence settled around us once more as it slowly grew darker.

"We should head home," I said after a while.

"Yeah, I'm starving," Skye grumbled as she got to her feet, and Cyrus quickly did the same.

Although I was the one to suggest we leave, I was hesitant to get to my feet. As much as I wanted to appear prepared for the conversation I had to have with my father, I was far from it.

Elinor

When I neared the front door of my house, I could clearly hear everyone's loud voices inside. Being that my house was also the packhouse, there were wolves around constantly.

I didn't mind it much, but I wished I had more privacy from time to time. With the keen hearing that all were-wolves had, a private conversation was never actually private.

I stepped into the house and removed my cloak.

A few wolves nodded in my direction, but as I made my way to the kitchen, the pack's Beta appeared before me, shaking his head.

I sighed as my shoulders dropped.

"He wants to see you," Connor informed me, holding his hand out for the rabbit and groceries I'd brought home. "He heard about what you did."

"I'm not surprised. News travels fast around here. So, where is he?"

"His office." He patted my shoulder before turning away. "Good luck."

I inhaled deeply as I watched him walk away, his long blond hair swaying against his back. Exhaling heavily, I headed back in the direction of the staircase. My footsteps on the wooden stairs echoed so loudly in my ears it distracted me from figuring out what I intended to say.

Finally, standing in front of my father's office, I took a deep breath, knocked on the door, and entered.

He stood up immediately, rising to his towering height of 6'7". Leaning forward, he placed his large hands on his desk, then shook his head. "What were you thinking, Elinor? How many times do I have to tell you to stop interfering with Guard business? I'm getting really tired of this."

"It would have been Guard business . . . if any of them had actually been there to begin with, Father." I sat down and angled my head towards my mother, who was looking out the window on the other side of the room. "Sorry I was late with dinner, Mother."

She smiled, her chin dimple becoming more pronounced. "It's okay, honey."

My father threw her a dark look.

She arched a brow at him. "What? Come now, Grayson, we've been over this how many times? I'm tired of arguing."

"And I'm tired of her not doing as I asked," he replied before looking my way, his green eyes narrowing angrily. "You have an image to uphold, Elinor. You're to be a Luna."

And there it was. I had hoped he wouldn't say it . . . but he had. "Oh, right, my image. I'm sorry, I'm not a dress-wearing, tea-drinking, do-everything-perfectly kind of girl. And *if* I become a Luna, I won't become that person, either. You might not want to accept who I am, Father, but with all due respect, that is not really my problem."

He stood up, his eyes growing even darker with anger.

I knew I had gone too far, but I would not back down now. Still, it didn't hurt to decrease the tension a bit, considering what I was about to ask him. "I tried not to intervene," I added softly. "But I knew the vendor, and nobody else was doing anything. I helped someone, Father. Why are you trying to make me feel bad about it?"

He exhaled and some of the tension in his eyes faded. While I inherited his green eyes, I had my mother's black wavy hair and creamy skin. My father, on the other hand, had dark brown hair and a natural tan.

"I'm not trying to make you feel bad, Elinor. What you did was a good thing. It's the werewolf way to help others. But you know it's not proper for a lady to straddle men while wearing a dress." He shook his head slowly in dismay.

"I'd be wearing pants if I was in the Werewolf Guard," I mumbled.

He threw his hands into the air and turned away. "I knew that was coming." He looked at my mother. "Speak to your daughter, Clarice."

"That's enough, Elinor," she chastised as she stepped forward, running her hand down her deep blue dress.

"So, I guess now is a bad time to ask if I can join the Werewolf Guard again, right?"

My father spun around to stare at me as if wondering where I got the gall to truly ask that. "For the last time, Elinor, you—"

"That's enough arguing, both of you." My mother held her hands up and closed her eyes, her annoyance clear. "Elinor, if you join the Guard, you will not be able to carry out your duties as Luna. Do you understand? If you don't stop getting into trouble, we're prepared to have you stay with Ivana for a few months."

My heart stopped. "You want to send me to Grandma? Are you kidding?"

She shrugged. "Since you refuse to listen to me or your father, I'm sure a few weeks with her will—"

"—kill me. A few weeks with her would kill me." My father's mother was the stern, no-nonsense type, and while I loved her and my grandfather, she was way too much to handle.

"She'll groom you into the perfect Luna," my mother added. She smiled as if her comment was funny.

I looked at her with betrayal in my eyes. "You're worse than he is," I told her. I turned to leave but paused before I made it to the door. "You know I'm capable of being Alpha.

And no, I'm not going to argue for the position, but you know I'd do well as a Guard. I'm capable of being so much more than just a Luna."

"Elinor, being Luna is an important role," my mother said, the hurt clear in her voice. "We offer help where needed. We stand by our Alpha. We help to build our family, our pack."

While my father and I had always had a strained relationship, I was close with my mother, and the last thing I wanted was to hurt her. But still, I wouldn't be swayed. I wouldn't come out and say Lunas were useless—although I sometimes secretly thought it—but I needed them to know it was just not what I wanted. "I know, Mother. But it's not for me." I turned to my father. "I want to be out there, fighting. I just wish you both could support me, instead of trying to make me into what *you* want."

"You're *my* daughter, you carry *my* name, and you'll do as I say. I won't let you ruin your life. And I won't let you put yourself in harm's way, either. That's final."

We stared at each other for a moment, my green eyes piercing his. Cyrus was right—my father was a stubborn man. I owe my own stubbornness to him, I suppose.

I straightened my spine and placed my right hand over my heart.

My father's face morphed with confusion.

"You're not just my father, but also my Alpha. And that's more important." I bent forward. "Goodnight."

"Elinor, please," my mother pleaded as she stepped forward.

"Goodnight," my father replied, his voice low. But I heard it—the nerve I'd struck. "We'll be visiting a neighboring pack tomorrow. You'll meet with the Alpha's firstborn to see if you're mates."

I'd dealt him a fine blow and he sent an even greater one right back at me. Biting down on my lip, I looked away, realizing I'd lost yet another battle with my father.

"And don't try to fight me on this. You're of age, Elinor, and we've put this off long enough. Finding your mate is a life-changing event. When you feel that connection, you'll realize that there's nothing better than being by your mate's side. You'll see the true importance of being a Luna to many wolves who'll look up to you." My father smiled. "It'll give you the purpose you so desperately seek—the right kind of purpose."

"Life-changing," I repeated under my breath, my jaws clenched. "The right purpose huh?"

I knew these conversations were stressful for my parents. It probably wasn't easy to have a firstborn daughter who refused to do what everyone expected of her, especially in something as important as this. But I only had one life to live, and I refused to let them dictate my future. It was *my* life, after all.

The *right* purpose?

Was he being serious?

Exhaling through my mouth, I turned and left without saying another word, my fists clenched as I fought back tears. If I'd been born a boy, we wouldn't even be having this conversation. I couldn't change my gender, but that didn't mean I'd let them force me into living a life I knew I'd hate. And if I couldn't be Alpha, then I wouldn't settle for anything less than becoming a Werewolf Guard.

2

ELINOR

I could see the bonfire blazing within the forest, and the closer I got to it, the more I yearned for a drink. Werewolves didn't get drunk easily using alcohol, but the local witches had created a special potion, an alternative drink that could induce the same intoxication experienced by humans.

I needed that right now.

"I thought you weren't coming," Skye exclaimed as she bounced over to me, a cup in hand.

I could tell she was already tipsy. I swiped the cup from her and downed the contents. Squeezing my eyes, I endured the burn as the liquid slid down my throat.

"Wow, I'm guessing your chat with your father didn't go very well." She took the empty cup back and sighed.

"It didn't," I grumbled. We moved over to the table that was set up with food and drink. "I'm going to see another pack in the morning."

Skye, who was in the process of filling her glass, froze.

"No," she drawled. "You're going to meet a male Alpha-born?"

I nodded.

She gave the cup to me before pouring just a little more. "Have a drink, honey."

I gulped down the warm drink. The more I drank, the more it burned, but it also felt so good. My tense shoulders relaxed somewhat as I lowered the cup from my lips.

"Well, well, well, if it isn't the Alpha-born," a voice crooned from behind me.

I grinned as I spun around.

Behind me stood a kitsune—a man capable of shifting into a fox. His clan was one of three that had moved to America from Japan.

"Well, well, well, if it isn't the shortest man I've ever seen," I teased. "Hello to you too, Zenko."

He gasped and placed his hand over his heart. "You wound me." His brown monolid eyes lowered as he pinned me with a curious stare. "Aren't you banned from drinking? Or partying? Or just . . . living in general? Haven't you joined the Guards yet?"

My brows furrowed.

Beside me, Skye sighed. "Shut up, Zenko, or she's going to—"

Her warning came too late. I kicked his leg out from under him and grabbed the cup in his hand as he fell.

Behind him, his friends erupted into laughter.

I put his cup to my lips and drained it. I smirked as he carefully got up. "You were saying?" I gave his cup back to him.

He stared into it with an impressed smile. "Alright then, I see how it is." He brushed his hand down his pants.

Cyrus approached us. "What are you guys doing?" he asked.

As Cyrus raised his cup to his lips, I snatched it and sauntered away, emptying it as well.

Behind me, Skye and the kitsune cheered me on before erupting into laughter.

Finally, I felt truly relaxed as I threw the cup over my shoulder. I knew Zenko was only messing around. He was known for his good-natured teasing, but tonight, well, he'd struck a nerve.

I hated how much others knew about my suffocating life.

"Hey, wait up!"

I paused and turned around.

Cyrus was jogging toward me. "Wait up," he repeated.

The moment he reached me, I started walking again.

"What's with all the drinking?" he asked.

"He said no again," I told him as I stopped and braced myself on the trunk of a tree.

The air felt warm from the towering bonfire, and although the atmosphere was filled with laughter and happiness, I wasn't feeling it. The drinks I'd consumed had lifted the tight feeling in my chest, but within my mind, my conversation with my parents kept playing over and over again.

At a young age, I accepted the fact that I would never be Alpha, but that was when my yearning to become more than just Luna had started. Because of my appearance and my lineage, people expected me to be the sweet little werewolf princess my father wanted me to be.

Screw being a damsel in distress.

"Tomorrow I have to meet another Alpha-born to see if we're mates. Tomorrow might be the beginning of the end for me."

"And what if he's not your mate?" Cyrus asked as he, too, leaned against the tree.

"Then I'll meet another Alpha-born, and then another, and another, until I find my mate." I shook my head at how tedious it all sounded to me. A werewolf's mate was predetermined by The Goddess—all that was left for us to do was meet. Still, it felt odd to know that at this very moment, my perfect other half was somewhere out there just waiting to meet me. "Who knows how long it will take?"

"And when there are no more Alpha-born werewolves for you to meet?" he questioned.

I sighed. "Then I suppose I'll have to meet werewolves who aren't Alphas, but who come from noble families. My father wants his bloodline to carry on, and other Alphas want the Blackmoon strength within their packs. It's like my only value is as a breeder. I just have to sit there, look pretty, behave myself, marry an Alpha, and push out the next generation of little entitled Alpha pups. Well, no thanks!"

"I'm sorry," Cyrus said, his voice almost a whisper. "I understand the burden your family is putting on you . . . more than you know."

I looked his way. "What's going on with you?"

A moment of silence passed between us before he combed his hair backward. "It's my mother. She wants me to take over the Legion she commands."

My eyes widened, but I dared not say anything.

Cyrus rarely spoke about his home or family, and who

could blame him? His mother was one of the seven deadly sins. The seven sins that plagued both humans and supernaturals were Pride, Lust, Greed, Gluttony, Sloth, Wrath, and Envy, and there were seven demons that were the personification of each sin. Cyrus, as the son of the sin Lust, was considered royalty in the Underworld.

"She wants me to stop spending so much time on Earth. She said I should start acting like royalty and not mingle so much with mortals." He rolled his eyes.

We stood in silence for a moment watching Skye and the others, their loud laughter filling our ears. "What are you going to do?" I asked him after the laughter died down.

He shrugged. "I was summoned home. I've been avoiding the trip for too long now, but I have a feeling this time that I'd better go before someone is sent to get me."

"Your mother will send someone after you? Like, someone that would hurt you?"

He shook his head. "No."

For all the years Skye and I had known Cyrus, we'd never seen his true side, the demon within him. We'd seen his wings and his gray eyes turn black but had never caught a glimpse of Cyrus: the sex demon feeding or using his powers.

Even though I was sad to hear what Cyrus was going through, it was nice to have a friend who could understand what kind of pressure I was facing. It looked like my parents weren't the only ones who didn't understand their child and tried to make their choices for them.

When I turned to Cyrus to speak, I found his gaze focused on Skye and one of Zenko's friends in an intense arm-wrestling match, one that she eventually lost. Cyrus's arms were crossed over his chest as he watched them.

Zenko's friend turned to give Zenko a high five, taking his eyes off Skye for a moment. But that was all it took for her to shift into her wolf. Some werewolves shift faster than others. Despite Skye's rather rough first change, she was one who shifted quickly.

Seconds later, she'd tackled him to the ground.

The crowd gathering around them erupted into cheers and whistles as the kitsune shifted into a bright orange fox, his fur illuminated by the bonfire.

Skye's dark brown wolf was three times the size of the fox, but he stood his ground as she attacked him, tackling him to the ground again.

From where we stood, we could hear people betting on who would win.

Beside me, Cyrus started to laugh. "There is no way I can ever leave you guys. You mean more to me than anyone else."

Cyrus has never been the overly affectionate type. We considered him the logical thinker out of the three of us, so his words meant more to me than he realized. I knew they were genuine. "Well, if you ever lose the battle with your mother and have to take over your clan, Skye and I can always visit," I suggested.

His head slowly turned my way. "Don't even joke about that. I'd rather you guys never saw that place." His brows pulled together. "I'm not the same person there that I am when I'm here."

I nodded. I'd seen that. The few times he'd visited the demon realm before, there'd been darkness cloaking him on his return. It was as if each time he went home, his true nature became more dominant. It made me wonder sometimes if his kindness was all an act.

But Skye and I knew the real Cyrus. He was just one of a kind.

"You're the only demon who has earned his place among us and is trusted," I told him. "That will never change because of where you come from."

He gave me a soft smile and returned to watching Skye's wolf, still locked in battle.

When the fight came to an end—with Skye the victor, of course—we went over and joined them.

After hanging out for a few more hours, Cyrus insisted on walking Skye and me home. We laughed and loudly chatted the entire time.

While I did my best to sneak into my house quietly, I think I might have knocked something over on the way upstairs. Once I got to my room, I had the best sleep I'd had in a long time, with no worrying thoughts of what I had to do the following day.

3

WILL

Without even needing to look outside the carriage, I could tell I'd entered Vampire Territory. The rank smell of death gave it away. For quite some time, this place had been my home, but I left after growing tired of it, tired of the deadness. Now it was the last place I wanted to be.

Wondering if it was as bad as I'd remembered it, I looked outside the window at the barren land, void of all signs of life. I would arrive just prior to daybreak just as I'd planned, which meant most members of the coven would be in their chambers. Vampires didn't have to sleep during the day, but they did have to avoid the sunlight. However, where I was headed, there were no windows of any kind, which meant a few vampires would still be wandering about.

If I could've stayed away much longer, I would've. Unfortunately, my mother was a persistent woman, and quite some time had passed since my last visit.

Whatever reason my mother had for summoning me back, I wasn't going to like it. I never did.

Thankfully, the time of day meant no guards outside to hassle with. With a few minutes to spare before daybreak, I saw to the carriage, then threw open the massive oak doors to the palace myself. The few vampires who were still out and about froze in their tracks, clearly stunned to see me. The heavy door thudded behind me, and I paused in the foyer.

The sight of the black walls illuminated by torches and the multiple sofas and red pillows thrown across the floor for lazy vampires to lounge all day and night transported me back in time. At one point, I'd spent most of my leisure time on those sofas. That was back when I'd adored living within these walls, being loved, feared, and worshipped.

Now, however, I was only feared, and I found I preferred it that way. It meant I was left alone to do as I pleased.

As I walked towards the stairs, all the vampires bowed until I passed them. I could hear their hushed whispers behind me. This was always how they behaved when I was around, but no longer cared about what they had to say about me at this point.

There were a few people here I definitely didn't want to see, so hopefully I could just speak to my mother as she'd requested and be on my way with as little drama as possible.

On the highest level was my mother's chamber and outside her door, like a few others on this level stood two guards in black armor and red masks, which covered their faces and left only their eyes visible. Unlike the lower floors, there was utter silence here.

All guards bowed as I passed, but none spoke.

I paused for a moment at a door that lead to my bedroom. There were guards posted outside it as well, but instead of going in, I continued on. I wouldn't be staying. But the second I entered my mother's chamber, I was hit with the smell of fresh blood.

I took a breath, inhaling the fruity scent of fae blood. I'd fed before embarking on this journey, but it would be time for me to feed again soon.

"Finally," a soft voice echoed through the grand room, rising to the high ceiling. "My boy is home."

"Temporarily," I answered as I looked around the room. "But hello, Mother."

She frequently changed the room's décor, and this time the walls were white to match the sheer curtains around her massive bed that could sleep several people comfortably. Large door to the right led to a balcony, where she often liked to spend her time.

Behind the sheer curtains surrounding the bed, I could see her, her black hair as dark as mine standing out against the contrasts of white pillows and sheets.

On either side of her were bodies, no doubt the source of the fresh blood I smelled, their heartbeat silent.

"I've missed you, William," she said. "It won't kill you to visit your loving mother more often."

Loving? As beautiful as my mother was, she was colder than any other vampire I knew and equally vicious. Like all vampires, love wasn't something she understood. Among vampires there was a sense of loyalty and devotion to an extent where other species might interpret it as love.

But love like other species experienced it—a sensation, from what I'd been told—wasn't something vampires understood.

I'd been trying to understand how love worked among

other other species. I'd experienced everything there was to experience cloaked in darkness, but there was more to learn. There had to be. It was a craving that had appeared abruptly, and it was the reason I no longer felt at home in these cold walls.

Because of it, other vampires held disdain for me. I'd always been different from them—very different.

"I would visit more often if you were the only one I had to see."

She chuckled, the sound playful. "Oh, don't worry about them. You loved this place once, but then you left." She sat up, and though she was somewhat hidden by the sheers, I turned away from her nakedness. "Where is my destroyer, William, my son whose savagery was once compared to the Demon King himself?"

I didn't answer.

"Okay, have it your way, then." Her tone hardened. "I'm sending you to Bronwen Coven, and before you think to object, it's not up for debate."

A hand reached around me from behind and pointy black nails the length of a finger slid across my cheek. Strands of my hair that fell below my shoulders slid through my mother's porcelain white fingers before she firmly held my shoulder.

"Does the coven need to be purged?" I asked, and she chuckled, the sound right by my ear. In another second, it was across the room.

"Oh no, no, no, the Bronwen Coven has loyal vampires, and if they needed to be punished in any way, that would be too lowly of a task for you. You and I have an affair to take care of with the nobles who govern the coven."

"What business do I have with the Bronwen Coven?"

"So many questions," she hissed, and my fists clenched. "I'll tell you all you need to know after you've had a drink with me, William. You leave tomorrow, but you know well enough that my business is yours. What is wrong with you? More so, have you forgotten that you'll be taking my place here someday?"

"With all due respect, you know how I feel about that," I grumbled, knowing this conversation would come up.

"And you know how I feel about it!" she yelled. Her voice was no longer beautiful but a guttural sound like an angry beast. It thundered around us, no doubt penetrating the walls. "You will do as I say! You will take my place!"

I didn't respond. It would only make matters worse to anger her further. No, I needed to remain calm and think rationally. For decades she'd reminded me at every turn that I would take her place here at this godforsaken place, and for decades I'd been opposed to the idea.

It had yet to happen, and I intended on keeping my distance to make sure it remained that way.

I was lucky she hadn't killed me the moment I first refused, but it was no secret that she favored me above all others. And I knew it didn't come from a mother's love for her son. No, it was because I was different from every other vampire before me—a fact that earned me nothing but hatred from the others. But to her . . . to her, I was her greatest creation.

Visiting the Bronwen Coven might not be such a bad idea if I played my cards right. Whatever business she had with the nobles, I'd handle it and then be on my way. I'd never visited that coven or the town close to it. I'd spent years travelling the earth, running from the responsibilities my mother continued to force on me, and Bronwen Coven would serve as another place for me to hide, for a while at least.

I'd heard the supernaturals in the town lived peacefully, more so than many other towns. So I could definitely make use of that to further understand the changes I'd been feeling.

"As you wish, Mother. I'll leave tomorrow," I said after some time, and her joyous laughter echoed through the room.

"There he is, my William! Never forget your place, my son. Now come, let's feast!"

4

ELINOR

The carriage shook as a wheel hit a stone on the rocky path, and my body jerked violently. I groaned with exasperation.

I remembered now the part I didn't like about drinking, which was why this was only the second time I'd ever been drunk. I definitely had a hangover—at least that was what the humans and witches called it. Every sound thundered through my head and the sunlight streaming in through my window this morning had set my eyes ablaze.

Now, riding with my parents and brother in the carriage with me, I kept my eyes closed, hoping for the horrible feeling to subside.

"I can't believe you chose to get drunk last night, of all nights, Elinor," my mother admonished.

I kept my eyes closed, trying to keep the contents of my stomach where they were. "It wasn't planned, Mother," I finally replied, cracking an eye open. "I'm fine. Or at least, I will be by the time we get there."

My father made an ominous sound.

I opened my other eye to look in his direction.

He stared at me. Though his face appeared void of emotion, his eyes were dark with anger.

Beside him, my little brother was sleeping soundly with his head on my mother's lap, his hair dark brown like our father's.

"You knew of our plans for today and the importance of them. You should have stayed home last night." He shook his head. "You need to act more responsibly, Elinor."

I sat up. "I'm fine."

"Oh, you're fine?" he repeated. "I can still smell the concoction those witches came up with on you. There's a chance that you're mated to Alpha Edon's son. How will it look that the future Luna of his pack is a drunk?"

I pressed my fingers to my temple. "A drunk? Are you serious? All I needed was one night to try to clear my mind. I'm not a drunk, and you know it." I shook my head, my anger making the hangover fade in comparison.

My mother placed her hand on his thigh while she continued to caress my little brother's head.

I didn't understand how Jackson managed to sleep so soundly, given our father's booming voice and the rocky journey.

"All I want is the best for you, Elinor. So don't you sit there and pretend this is something so casual."

"And what about what I want, Father? What about what I think is best for me? Does my opinion about my own life not count for anything?" I tilted my head to the side, staring at him. "You know I'm capable of being a great Guard, or even an Alpha, for that matter. I have what it takes. However, as I've told you, I've accepted the fact that I cannot lead the pack, so why deny me the only other wish I have? There are already women in the Guard, so being female isn't an issue."

"You have to be mated to an Alpha-born or someone from a noble family—that is the way things are for people like us. Being a Guard is an honorable job, but it's not for you."

"And if I don't agree to be married off?" The words slipped from my lips before I could stop them. "If I'm not mated to an Alpha-born or noble, what then father? Will I be disowned?"

"Elinor, that's enough," my mother interjected sternly, obviously seeing my father's brows furrow and his color rise. "Let's not borrow trouble. Besides, you know, it's expected for Alpha-borns to be mated. The chances of you not finding your mate are slim. Can we end this argument? Jackson's sleeping."

I said nothing further as I gazed down at the pale blue dress my mother had picked out for me. Pink rose quartz gems were knitted around the neckline and waist, so they served as a good distraction to avoid looking at my father.

I hadn't asked an unreasonable question--at least, I didn't think it was. The way my father behaved, it was as if he believed if I didn't find a mate, I might die or single-handedly ruin our family's image.

It was the same thing he feared about me becoming a Werewolf Guard. Because I was a firstborn, the role I was to play in life had been set out for me the moment I was born. And because I was a female firstborn, Jackson's life course had also been set.

I glanced at my mother.

She reached over to my father and removed fuzz from his hair.

He smiled at her warmly, took her hand, and kissed the back of it.

I smiled a little at the affection shared between them. I didn't completely hate the thought of finding my mate—not when I had my parents as an example of how beautiful life could be with a significant other.

What I feared was—losing myself. I'd seen how much my mother dedicated herself to my father. I understood this was what love was like because he did the same for her, but I wasn't ready to put my dreams aside to become a wife.

Why couldn't I be the first Alpha-born woman to not become a Luna?

We continued on our journey in silence for the most part, until my brother Jackson woke up. Because he rarely left the pack grounds, he found this little trip to be fun.

Personally, I'd rather be buried alive.

Jackson and I had never been close. I certainly didn't dislike him—he was my brother, after all. But he was old enough to understand why he was to be Alpha, even though he was the second born. Sometimes when Father and I argued in his presence, I would see him look at me with regret, which made me feel horrible.

None of this was his fault. It was just the way things were.

Elinor

I stepped out of the carriage and inhaled the smell of the trees surrounding us. I wanted to bend backward and crack my aching back but refrained from doing so when Father pinned me with a quick glare.

Our journey had been a rocky one because the Midnight Crescent Pack lived deep in the woods.

"Clarice, it's been too long!" a petite woman exclaimed as she opened her arms wide to hug my mother. "Is this really Jackson? The last time I saw you, boy, you barely had teeth."

"I have lots of them now," Jackson replied proudly.

My parents laughed along with the woman, who I assumed must be the Luna of this pack.

"Thanks for having us, Komina. It's been too long," my mother told her. "And this is Elinor, our eldest."

Komina's smile stretched so wide, I thought it would physically meet her ear. She moved her light—almost platinum—blond hair behind her ear as she looked me up and down. "Gosh, girl, turn, let me look at you. Oh, Clarice, she's stunning," she gushed to my mother as I turned in a circle.

My mother's cheeks turned bright red. "Thank you. She gets it from me, of course," she added with a chuckle.

The door to their home opened, and a man stepped out, followed by three younger men. Although Komina had platinum blond hair, only one of her sons had inherited it. But he also had his father's brown eyes, instead of her pale blue ones.

Behind him were two other men—twins—their hair a dirty blond like their father's, along with his brown eyes.

"Clarice, Grayson!" The man's voice boomed around us as he greeted my parents. "Welcome, welcome."

I glanced at the three younger men, seeing their eyes roam up and down my body. I tried not to sigh with relief.

I'm not mated to any of them. If I were, they'd be on me in seconds.

"Thank you for your invitation, Marcus. Although I think if none of your sons has reacted just yet, then I'm afraid my daughter isn't mated to any of them." My father voiced my thoughts as he looked at me and then at the men.

Alpha Marcus turned to look at me, a soft smile on his lips. Where my father was tall and muscular, Alpha Marcus matched his height but was more on the plump side with a round belly. "That's unfortunate because she is quite beautiful, but no matter. You're all welcome to stay the night and rest before returning home. We'll be having a gathering tonight." He held his meaty hand out to his sons. "This is Annik," he introduced, pointing to the one with the platinum blond hair. "He's my firstborn. Behind him are Landon and Leecan."

After the introductions were over, we made our way inside. The guys kept looking at me, but I did my best to avoid their gaze. I might not be mated to any of them, but I wasn't interested in being hit on by any of them, either.

I felt grateful for Luna Komina when she invited my mother and me to join her and a few other women while the men went off to have a private chat. The worst had passed, thankfully.

However, my father made it a point to give me a stern warning before walking off. "Behave yourself," he warned, which earned me curious stares from the guys.

I gave him a sweet smile and turned away. It was funny how I was being told to behave myself—not Jackson—as if I was the young, mischievous one in the family.

Walking inside, I was stunned by the way this family had incorporated nature into their home. A massive tree root was the centerpiece of the house.

Alpha Marcus, obviously noticing my surprise, had explained that the house itself had been built around the tree and that the wolf who had brought together the Midnight Crescent Pack was buried beneath it.

"Unfortunately, you aren't mated to any of our boys," a voice said, cutting through my thoughts.

I blinked rapidly. "Um, yes, quite," I replied softly.

Three women had just entered the room, and I wasn't sure which of the three had spoken to me.

Luna Komina introduced my mother and me to her sister, cousin, and friend, but I honestly couldn't remember which was which. The only one I was sure of was Luna Komina's sister, who shared her platinum blond locks and pale blue eyes.

My mother placed her hand on my leg. "It's a shame they weren't mates, but maybe someday, a daughter of Elinor's will be mated to an Alpha from the Midnight pack. That would be something."

"Gosh, Clarice, I remember when you came here to meet Marcus's brother," Komina laughed.

Once more, I tuned them out. I found comfort in the gems on my dress and smiled from time to time without really hearing what they were talking about. This, *this* was exactly what I didn't want, I thought, as their conversation gradually shifted into gossip. I wanted to be outside training, or reading about battles long ago fought, or learning how to defeat dark creatures.

My mother wasn't born a firstborn, but Komina was, just like me. Yet, here she was, serving tea when I knew she had enough strength to match any Alpha.

My lips parted as I was about to ask to be excused when the door opened.

Annik walked in. He wasn't wearing a shirt any longer, revealing a deep scar running from his left pec to his shoulder.

I tilted my head to the side somewhat as I admired him. He stood over six feet with impressive muscles like most werewolves, but funny enough, it was his scar that intrigued me. How had he gotten it?

"The twins and I are going hunting for the party tonight," he informed his mother, his voice surprisingly soft.

She nodded. "Sure."

"Can I go as well?" I blurted out.

The room fell silent.

"I think it would be best if you let them go ahead without you," my mother quickly replied as my father and Marcus walked into the room.

Marcus walked forward and patted Annik's shoulder. "Now, now, although they aren't mated, I think it's a good idea for them to get to know each other. A bond between them will be beneficial to both packs in the future."

Annik looked my way, and I held his stare. His eyes narrowed as I refused to look away, so I narrowed mine as well.

Two could play this game.

The side of his mouth twitched upwards with a smirk. "I agree." Annik turned to my father and then me. "Shall we?"

My father nodded.

Alpha Marcus clapped his hands. For an Alpha, he was certainly very perky. Alphas tended to not show much emotion—they needed their hard exterior to keep order.

"There is a room just through there where you can shift, if you don't wish to do it here," Komina told me.

I thanked her and walked away.

Werewolves ended up in the nude more often than they wore clothes at times, but more so for men. It was not common for a werewolf to be shy of their appearance—and I wasn't—but I'd rather not strip down and stand naked in front of my parents and everyone else when no one else was shifting. It felt too much like I had an audience.

It had been a little while since my last shift. As I removed my dress and inhaled deeply, I called on my slumbering wolf. She awoke instantly. As she did, my green eyes changed to black. I closed them for a moment as my fangs pierced through my gums and my nails elongated.

The pain was mild and could easily be ignored, but it increased as my knee snapped backward. I fell to the ground on my hands and allowed the feeling of my bones breaking to wash over me. It always felt like something beneath my skin was trying to break free, shifting, and moving beneath my flesh.

My skin started to sprout fur and my hands turned into feet as I released myself to my wolf.

Once done, I stretched outward on my front paws and shook myself, smiling inwardly. Being in my true form always left me feeling so relaxed. My strength doubled, and my senses heightened. I was who I was meant to be.

I clawed at the door.

Marcus opened it and stared at my wolf with wide eyes as I exited the room.

I had expected his response. It was the same one I always got when people saw my wolf. This had been the reason I hadn't been allowed to shift around anyone who was not from my pack. And the reason . . . ?

Werewolves tended to have dark fur. Only I didn't. My fur was blinding white. Wolves with white fur were rare—so rare as to be mythical. Their existence was based on stories of the first werewolf, a direct descendant of our Goddess— who was said to have had a white coat, signifying purity.

So, from time to time, whenever a wolf was born with a light-colored coat, people believed that the wolf had received the Goddess's blessing.

Annik, who had been sporting a smug expression earlier, looked shocked.

However, my father's pride was evident in his eyes.

"She's gorgeous," Komina whispered as she stepped forward and then stopped. She looked at my parents. "I understand why you've tried to keep her locked away, but now I'm even more disappointed that she won't be joining our clan. I've never seen a wolf with white fur."

"Well, she has some light gray fur too, to be frank," my mother clarified nervously.

Komina waved her hand dismissively. "She's pure white. We can all see that," Komina added.

I shook my head. One more reason I was rarely permitted to shift—I'd have to deal with hearing all of this purity talk from people who thought my white coat indicated I was closer to the Goddess.

Even though I did believe in and honor our Goddess, I did not care for this kind of talk at all—or the unwanted attention it brought with it.

I walked over to Annik, who still looked stunned, and bumped his leg, eager to leave the room.

Finally, we made our way outside to where his brothers were waiting.

As we approached them, they looked from me to Annik and then back again in shock.

One of them pointed at me, the twin with a faint scar to the right of his upper lip.

Annik nodded his head before his brother could voice his thoughts. "Yup, you see correctly. Let's go." He started to shift.

His brothers gave me one last look before doing the same.

Annik's wolf was deep beige, while the twin wolves had almost identical black and rust fur. They walked ahead of Annik and me, their noses to the air.

I could hear other werewolves in the distance, no doubt members of their pack, but the further we ventured into the woods and the thicker the forest got, the more the sounds faded.

Soon enough, I caught the scent of a deer in the wind. The twins must have detected it first because they suddenly ran off.

Annik reacted immediately, bounding forward as well.

There was no way I would be left behind, so I followed them, snapping tree limbs as I picked up speed. My claws dug into the earth, pushing myself forward, and within seconds, I passed Annik.

Ahead of the twins were two deer, their long legs propelling them over large stones and broken branches.

The scent of humans suddenly slammed into me.

Annik howled to his brothers, signaling them to stop. But they kept chasing the deer.

Behind me, Annik growled loudly, and he suddenly shot past me. He snapped his jaw at me as he ran by, warning me to stay put.

I slowed down.

If there were humans so deep in the forest, they had to be hunting. Meeting hunters right now, even if they were only trying to catch a meal, might not go well.

Humans lived alongside supernaturals fairly peacefully . . . unless laws were broken or territories were entered without permission.

Why am I standing here?

I bared my teeth, suddenly irritated. I wasn't the type of girl—or wolf—to sit back and be *protected*. I ran in the direction where Annik and the twins had vanished, my nostrils flaring as I followed their scent. Angry growls and snarls met my ears . . . as well as the raised voices of two men.

I sped up, my paws thundering on the forest floor. When I found them, one man had his sword raised at one of the twins. I burst from the trees and charged at the man, my growl echoing to the top of the trees.

The deer we were chasing were both on the ground, an arrow in each animal. One was dead, but the other was still alive, breathing faintly.

The man fell backward in fright, his sword falling out of his hand.

Beside him, the other man raised his bow and arrow.

I dodged to the side quickly as an iron-tipped arrow flew my way. I held my head low and bared my teeth, snarling at the two men.

Annik appeared by my side where he had been standing before his brothers, an arrow in the ground just a foot in front of him.

No doubt, the humans had been trying to hold them back from taking the deer, even though I could hear the thundering of their hearts from where I stood.

I snapped my jaw at the man, and he dropped the bow and arrow. I stepped forward quickly, and he fell backward as I stepped on the bow, breaking it.

With both men down, their heartbeats thundering in my ears, I noticed for the first time just how skinny they were. Their clothes were in shreds and dirty. The one who'd been holding the bow and arrow looked to be relatively young.

They're hungry.

Annik's growl had the boy wincing as he closed his eyes and turned his head to the side. I bit at Annik and growled low before walking towards the larger of the two deer, who cried out in panic.

Biting down on the animal's neck, I threw it towards the man and boy.

They stared at me in confusion for a moment.

I exhaled heavily as I shook my head.

One of the twins made a sound behind me, no doubt confused as to why I was giving them one of the deer, but I didn't respond.

The boy got to his feet hesitantly, his watery blue eyes staring at me in wonder, before picking up the deer with his father's help.

Then I turned away, stepping over the other deer, and headed back to the house.

5

CYRUS

When I stepped inside through the large double doors to my mother's castle, I was instantly met by low moans and intertwined whispers. I walked slowly, my hands in my pockets as I made my way up the blood-red carpeted staircase.

Half-naked demons were lounging around everywhere I looked, their black eyes on me as I passed by. The red light my mother insisted on having on at all times was enhancing the sexual atmosphere throughout the castle, but I supposed that was her goal.

Music drifted through the air. The soft eerie voice of a woman singing was the only thing I liked about this place.

Being an incubus, I shared the urges all these other demons felt. I knew the cravings they had. I knew the thirst and need that haunted them, but hell, I could control myself. Did they all need to act so out of control? I walked by four demons tangled together on the floor and pinned a succubus, a female sex demon, with a glare as she reached out to me.

She merely smiled, no doubt turned on by my rejection.

By the time I made it to my mother's office, I'd refused too many sexual invitations to count and had to break a demon's arm. I opened the door without knocking and walked in. My mother jumped up from behind her desk.

"My boy!" she cried with glee. "My beautiful boy's home!" She suddenly vanished from behind her desk and immediately re-appeared before me.

I allowed her to pull me into a brief hug before pulling away. "How are you, Mother?" I inquired.

She stepped away to look at me with a wide smile. Her wavy obsidian hair fell all the way to her knees. Though most succubi were tall with long legs, my mother was only 5'5" with wide hips and a cute, round face. She reached out and cupped my cheek, her hands ice cold. "Happy now that you're here," she smiled, looking to her left. "Are you two going to welcome your brother home?"

I followed her eyes and saw my half-brother and half-sister staring at me with hatred. Nothing new there.

"You never hug us like that," my half-sister Marinka grumbled as she uncrossed her long legs. She ran a hand up her slick high ponytail and moved her blond hair over her shoulder as she smirked at me. "Sup, big bro?"

"Marinka," I said in a low, disinterested voice.

My mother cleared her throat as she glared at my half-brother, Baxton.

He rolled his honey gold eyes. "Sup," he mumbled almost inaudibly.

I turned to my mother without responding.

Baxton—the sadistic prick—was my eldest brother and my least favorite of my many, many siblings. He also hated my guts because our mother chose me to be her successor and not him.

Hell, he could have her throne. I didn't want it.

"Why do you insist on hiding your wings?" My mother pushed her crimson-painted bottom lip out as she pouted. "You know I simply adore your wings. They remind me of your father."

I had always been impressed by just how much she was able to fake her emotions. Her gold eyes, like Baxton's, looked utterly sad, but it was all an act. I knew she was hollow. I ground my teeth as she turned away to walk back to her desk. I suddenly noticed that sitting in front of her desk were two humans—two females who appeared to be twins.

My mother reached out to them, and they crawled to her with love in their eyes. "Leave us, my pets. Go get something to eat and rest," she told them.

Both women, wearing nothing but their bras and under-wear, nodded and got to their feet.

"Return in three hours. Don't make me come find you myself."

They both kissed my mother before walking towards me to leave the room. They ran their hands down my chest, the heady scent of their arousal hitting me.

I ignored it. "Valencia, can you please tell me why I was summoned, so I may leave?" I inquired as soon as they left.

My mother sat down behind her desk, her face becoming serious. "Do not call me Valencia. I'm your mother." This time when she spoke, her voice wasn't soft and angelic but deep and contorted. Then she smiled sweetly. "And I missed my son. Is it not okay for me to miss my child?"

I stared at her blankly.

She soon began to chuckle.

From a young age, I figured out how to travel between worlds, and after many failed attempts, I finally got it right. The third night after arriving on Earth, I met Skye and Elinor. They'd been my family ever since, even though I'd had to return home from time to time.

Valencia wasn't the motherly type—she never had been and never would be. I had a different father than all my other siblings—which was why I had wings and most of the rest of them didn't—but he was never around, either. I think I'd met the man twice, and that was it.

"Your son?" Baxton suddenly laughed. "He's barely one of us and is rarely here. He's no son of yours, Mother, and you need to accept that." His eyes drifted to me. "He thinks he's better than us. He always has."

"I don't just think it—I know it," I quipped.

His face twisted with anger.

Beside him, Marinka chuckled, entertained by the bickering. She'd always thrived on chaos.

But this wasn't the reason I'd come here.

"So you think that just because you live among mortals, you're better than us?" Baxton tipped his head back and laughed. "Being around them has made you weak. How can you call yourself an incubus? Are you still a virgin, Cyrus? Be honest now."

"Virgin or not, I'm still the one who will inherit Mother's throne. What makes you think your words can affect me?" Sure, I didn't want the throne, but the threat was enough to shut up my older brother.

He jumped to his feet, obviously itching for a fight.

My shirt ripped as scarlet red wings sprouted from my back. My eyes changed to black.

He stopped in his tracks.

"There they are," my mother crooned in a low voice as she swung a leg onto her desk. "Sit down, Baxton."

His jaws visibly clenched, he stomped out of the room, shutting the door behind him. I noticed he closed it softly enough to avoid angering Valencia.

I folded my wings behind me.

"Your father is having a ball, and I'd like you to go with me," my mother explained.

Finally, here was the real reason I'd been called here. I shook my head. "I think I'll pass, Mother. I'm not interested in attending any parties thrown by the Demon King." I turned to leave.

Yes, I was the son of the Demon King—one of his many children—which solidified my role as royalty, not just as a child of a Sin.

Suddenly, I felt her nails dig into my shoulder. Before I knew it, she spun me around until I was facing her direction again. Mother's golden eyes burned bright as she glared at me. "Don't you dare turn your back to me. This isn't a request. You *will* be attending your father's ball, and that's final." She released my shoulder. "Like it or not, you're the King's son, and you need to act like it. You need to spend time with your own kind, Cyrus. Though you've trained yourself well on your own—your strength can't be denied— you need to remain here to reach your full potential. There is nothing for you among the mortals."

"You speak ill of them, yet you keep two with you here in the Underworld," I argued.

She shrugged. "They are pets, Cyrus, nothing more. You know feeding on humans and supernaturals is better than feeding on our own."

We stood in silence for a moment, and her eyes stopped glowing.

I sighed. If I didn't attend this party, my absence would be seen as an insult to the King, even though he probably didn't even remember I existed. "I'm sorry, Mother. I have things I need to take care of. The King won't notice my absence, I promise you that." I turned to leave, but her next words stopped me in my tracks and caused my blood to run cold.

"Fine, Cyrus. Enjoy your time with the werewolves you love so much," she purred softly. "They won't be around for much longer."

I turned to narrow my eyes at her. I moved toward her, not believing what I'd heard. I towered over her, trying to intimidate her. Even with her blood and my father's running through my veins, I knew I was nowhere as strong as she was. "What are you talking about?"

"What's so special about them, son? Tell me why you've chosen to live among those people instead of your own?"

I stared at her for a moment. She was a brilliant woman, strong and cunning. So why would she ask me something so foolish?

"I wasn't accepted as a child. Even by you," I admitted. Her eyes darkened for a moment, but I didn't care, so I continued, "I appeared weak, not enough like an incubus, and more importantly, not like my father. *Those people* raised me. A pack of wolves accepted a demon."

I made sure to emphasize the word *wolves*, so she'd understand exactly what I was saying. Leaving the Demon

Realm all those years ago, totally unprepared for the human world, had been dangerous. I should have died, and without the Blackmoon Pack, I probably would have. I stayed with them all these years because they were my family—my true family.

She patted my cheek and turned away. The sheer silver dress she wore dragged on the ground behind her as she returned to her desk.

I sighed and turned towards the door again. She didn't understand. Why was I surprised?

"See you at the ball, Brother. Make sure you feed before you attend. You're looking a little undernourished," Marinka shouted after me as I slammed the door shut behind me.

Elinor

A mother with her son stopped by the clinic just as I'd come by to wait on Skye. It was past the time for Skye to leave, and she stayed back an hour to help her mentor look after the little boy. After Nurse Hilary's initial assessment, Skye was allowed to provide care for him on her own.

The boy had yet to go through his first change, so he didn't heal as quickly as he would have if he'd already learned to shift. Skye bandaged his leg carefully, talking to him to distract him from the pain. Under Nurse Hilary's guidance, Skye had vastly improved in her training to become a pack doctor.

She glanced my way quickly and winked. I smiled. After

returning from the Midnight Crescent Pack an hour ago, I was eager to tell her everything that had happened.

A door to my right swung open, and a girl with dark blond hair cut just below her ears walked out. She grinned wide as she saw me and came over. I slid down on the bench to make room for her.

"Ione, shouldn't you be meditating or something?" I teased.

She threw me an annoyed look. Ione was our Enchanted, a werewolf unable to shift into a wolf but capable of seeing into the future and the minds of others. Some Enchanteds were even powerful enough to cast spells similar to the way witches could.

However, Ione was only fourteen years old, so she was not our official Enchanted just yet. But it wouldn't be long. Her mother, Nurse Hilary, kept a close watch on Ione to ensure nothing distracted her from her Enchanted studies. Being an Enchanted was a huge responsibility—almost as huge as being an Alpha.

"A break won't hurt." She sighed. "I've been up since before dawn. I'm exhausted."

"Why were you up so early?" I inquired.

She shrugged. "Bad dreams," she whispered as she brushed her hair from her eyes. Her brows knitted as she watched the little boy chatting with Skye. Then, suddenly, her eyes rolled back in her head.

My eyes widened in fright as I watched her. "Ione?" I called, then turned to Skye. But no one was paying attention. "Ione?"

"The full moon," Ione whispered, her head tilting to the side. "Be still on the full moon, or blood will rain onto our land. Be still on the full moon, and death won't follow . . ." She gasped for breath.

Finally, Skye looked our way.

My heart hammered inside my chest. This was the first time I'd ever seen Ione use her powers. *Did she just have a vision? What the hell did any of that mean?*

I tried to recall when the next full moon would be but would have to ask Skye or my mother to confirm. No, I'd ask Skye. My mother would only lecture me that forgetting was careless. Wolves were unable to shift during a full moon but my parents never allowed me to stray too far from the pack except to go into the town even without there being a full moon.

So I'd never felt concerned however, for other wolves it was best to be on guard in case a dark creature, like vampires tried to make use of their weakness.

Our pack had never been attacked but father always warned everyone to be careful.

But after what I'd just heard, as unclear as it was I felt uneasy.

"What did I just say?" Ione asked.

I shook my head as I tried to appear calm. "Nothing. Ah, you were telling me you had a nightmare, so you've been up since before dawn."

"Oh." She frowned as she placed a finger to her temple. "Right."

"Ione!" a familiar voice echoed through the clinic.

Ione sighed.

The door she had come through was thrown open, and her mother walked out, a large book in her hand. "You won't learn if you don't study, Ione. Stop bothering Elinor and go."

"See you around," she said sadly as she got up. She took the book from her mother and disappeared behind the door.

I felt terrible for the poor girl. I understood exactly how she felt.

"Hey, Elinor," Hilary greeted me, her dark blond hair in a high bun, with not a strand out of place. "So, I'm guessing you didn't find your mate, huh?"

I really hate how fast news travels around this place. "Um, no, not yet. How's Ione doing?"

Hilary sighed. "She's coming along well with her studies, and she can remember some of her visions now. The only issue we're having is her nightmares."

I nodded. "Yeah, she mentioned that just now."

"Unfortunately, she can't remember them once she wakes up. She'll scream and cry in her sleep and then forget everything as soon as her eyes open. I hate it. I wish I could make them stop." Hilary's eyes filled with tears for a moment.

I stood up and placed my hand on her shoulder. "Ione's a tough kid."

"All done," Skye announced, pulling her hair out of its bun as she approached us. "Ms. Jackson wants to speak with you, though," she alerted Hilary. Then she grinned. "Am I done for the day?"

"Yes, you did well. I'll see you tomorrow." Hilary waved goodbye to us and went to check on her other patients.

Skye pinned me with a look. "Let's go." She went over to pick up her old wool bag. "Tell me everything!"

Elinor

"*A*nnik sounds hot. If you don't want him, I'll take him." Skye laughed.

I shook my head at Skye as we made our way back home through the forest. I hadn't left out any details as I recounted the hunt I'd had with the guys and the party that had followed later that night.

During the party, Annik approached me. He told me he'd been angry at first but soon understood why I'd left the deer for those humans. They were poor and obviously in need. He wanted to let me know he was impressed with the way I'd handled the situation, that I'd stood my ground instead of standing on the sidelines. He'd even said he admired that kind of courage. He admitted it wasn't something he'd ever seen in other women from noble families. We had talked for a while and flirted a little, but that was as far as it went.

"On to the next one," I grumbled.

Skye pouted. "When are you leaving to visit the next pack?"

I shrugged. "I'm not sure. Father will let me know."

She leaned over to me. "Can I come this time? I mean, maybe I can pitch the idea to your mother that you need a maid or something." She held her head back as the sun pierced through the roof of trees above us. "I need to get away from this pack, even if it's just for a day."

"When Cyrus gets back, I'll ask Mother if we can go to that cabin we used to visit when we were kids. If Cyrus is there, she'll convince Father to let us go."

"It's funny when you think of it, isn't it? Your father won't let you join the Guard, but it's fine for you to go to a cabin alone with a sex demon." Skye shook her head.

I did the same. "Cyrus is a good guy—everyone knows that. He would never let any harm come to us, much less be the cause of it. Speaking of Cyrus, I wonder how he's doing," I said more to myself.

"I wish I knew," Skye muttered.

As we stepped onto the road to my house, someone yelled my name.

"Elinor, are you heading home?" Before us, Rin—a member of our pack—walked briskly toward us, her raven hair blowing in the wind. "You should probably hurry and sneak in through the back. You can't show up looking like that."

I gave her a look of confusion, then glanced down at my green dress, which had a few stains on the front. "What are you talking about?"

As she came to a stop before us, she frowned. "You haven't heard?"

I sighed. "No, I haven't, but the fact that I'm supposed to look presentable for it doesn't give me a good feeling about it. Please tell us what has you so excited."

"There is an Alpha at your house right now. He has business with your father, but his son came with him. I heard from one of the maids that he's gorgeous!" She walked around us. "Your father announced we'd be having a pack dinner tonight, so I need to go get a new dress. See you there." She continued in the direction of the town.

I started to back up, turning to walk back into the forest.

Skye grabbed my arm. "Why are you running?"

I gave her a dead stare. "Are you kidding? I just met an Alpha-born yesterday, and now I have to meet another one today? I need a minute to breathe, to prepare. What if this one is my mate?"

"Do you really want your father to send Guards looking for you?"

Pinching the bridge of my nose, I was about to say yes.

Her hold on me tightened. "Let's just go, Elinor. There is no point in hiding. You have to go home at some point, and I'm starving."

"So, because you're hungry, you want to put me through possibly meeting my mate and having my life as I know it come to an end?"

She yanked on my arm, her dark skin glowing in the sunlight. "Yes. I want to see this gorgeous Alpha-born myself."

"I swear, Skye, you need to think about other things besides food and men."

She turned to look at me as her eyes squinted with confusion. "What else is there?"

6

———

ELINOR

*D*inner had been truly a nerve-wracking experience. The Alpha-born to the Fairwater Pack, Nolan, wasn't my mate.

Thank the Goddess.

However, even I had to admit, Nolan was as gorgeous as Rin had described. His brown skin gave him the appearance of having the perfect golden tan. And with his light brown hair and piercing hazel eyes . . . *Phew!* Whispers about his good looks spread quickly, so even before dinner, girls were arriving at the packhouse.

Tonight, there would be a gathering in the woods. It would be just a get-together—not a party—where we could all enjoy the chilly night's air and the company of our fellow wolves. The packhouse was open, so anyone who wanted to could join and feast with us before the gathering.

Of course, this time around, there were more women present than men.

"This is unfortunate," Alpha Eli said to my father as they headed towards the stairs. He had spent a lot of time over

56

dinner sizing me up, then eying his son Nolan. "She would have been a strong Luna. I can see that."

"Yes, she would have, my friend. You're right," my father replied as they made their way to the second floor. "She still will be when she finds her mate and fixes her attitude. Sadly, she gets it from me."

"She's not the first wolf to be terrified of finding their mate. Her feelings will change when she finally finds him or when he finds her," Alpha Eli answered kindly.

I gritted my teeth.

That's exactly what I am afraid of.

Behind me, Nolan was surrounded by girls, all of whom were questioning him about his pack and what it was like living by the sea. The Fairwater Pack was the only pack known to live near the ocean, although they still had the forest at their backs. They'd made a name for themselves, even among the humans, because of their booming fishing business.

I turned and went upstairs to my room to freshen up before heading into the forest. I opened my trunk where I stored my cloaks and decided to wear a light brown one my mother had made for me many moons ago. Nolan and I hadn't spoken to each other just yet, but I was sure we would, eventually. Although, now that I thought about it, even with those girls clinging to him, he barely spoke.

A man of few words, huh?

I made my way outside and pulled my cloak closer to my body. The loud chatter of pack members filled the air as I inhaled the scent of the forest. I could always count on the smell of the trees and the earth to still my troubled mind.

Alpha Eli's words simply wouldn't stop replaying in my

mind. As strong as my love might be for my mate, if or when I ever met him, I refused to allow myself to change. Or maybe Alpha Eli meant that my outlook on having a mate might change once I experienced what it was like?

Either way, I was happy with the way things were now.

The trees were lit up by multiple stick lamps, the light from the flames casting a soft glow throughout the forest. Wolves were all together, some with a drink in hand, chatting amongst themselves.

It didn't take long for me to spot Nolan—there were girls everywhere around him. But what did surprise me was who he was talking to. The passive, good-looking young man I'd first seen was now smiling and talking animatedly to Skye.

Her head fell back as she laughed.

A few of the girls nearby definitely weren't happy. I stopped walking and decided to hang around to watch. I wasn't focusing on Nolan and Skye's conversation—I didn't want to invade their privacy—but I was sure the rest of those girls were listening closely to the entire thing. Practicing selective hearing would've been the polite thing to do, but I doubted they could resist a target as tempting as Nolan.

A loud thud echoed behind me, and I turned around.

Cyrus's large wings were disappearing into his back as he walked forward.

I felt my face light up, and a feeling of relief washed over me now that he was back. He always gave me the best advice, and right now, I could use some. I felt as if my father had trapped me on a marriage-go-round, an endless circle where I just met one man after another.

"Hey," he greeted me.

As he got closer, though, my smile slowly faded. "Hey," I murmured.

His voice sounded dull and void of emotion, and the kindness usually present in his eyes had given way to hardness. His face looked stony, and his energy felt off—dark. This was what I hated. He got this way every time he returned from his home.

Time in the Underworld was different than here on Earth, from what I understood. For us, it had only been a few days, but who knew how long it had been for him.

He frowned after a moment.

I followed his gaze.

He was staring at Skye and Nolan. As Nolan talked animatedly, a deep guttural sound came from Cyrus. It was a growl but a contorted one—the sound that demons made.

"His name is Nolan," I told him. "He's an Alpha-born my father invited here to see if he's my mate."

His eyes narrowed. "I'm assuming he's not?"

I shook my head. "He's not." I cleared my throat. "Um, are you okay? You always seem a little different after going home."

His eyes slid to me. He inhaled deeply and exhaled through his mouth. "I'm fine," he answered softly, but the look in his eyes as he watched Skye and Nolan suggested otherwise.

Cyrus had never given any of us a reason to fear him, to fear the demon within him, even though we knew it was there. But each time he went home, I was reminded of who he really was—demon royalty.

Skye turned to look our way. Her face lit up when she

spotted Cyrus, and she immediately told Nolan she'd be right back.

In turn, he looked our way. It was clear the way his brow rose when he saw Cyrus what was about to happen. And this was the worst possible time.

Demons didn't regularly hang out with other supernaturals, so Nolan had to be wondering why Cyrus was here. Despite Skye telling him she'd be right back, he walked with her.

I sighed.

Please don't let this turn into a fight.

My thought was forgotten when the force of a strong wind pushed me away from Cyrus. His red wings, spanning at least twenty feet, flapped once before he suddenly shot upwards into the sky.

"Cyrus!" Skye yelled, but within seconds, he'd vanished. She looked at me and sighed. "What was that?"

"You know how it is when he gets back." I glanced at Nolan and then back at her. "I'm sure he'll be fine."

Chewing on her lip, she rubbed at her temple. "Maybe I should go after him."

"Why was there a demon here?" Nolan asked as he glanced from me to Skye. He looked around, but no one seemed to care that a winged demon had just flown away from the gathering.

"I'm going to go look for him, okay?" Skye informed me. "I'll see you guys later." She walked off before Nolan could speak.

I sighed.

Skye and Cyrus had always had a special bond. No doubt, she was extremely worried about him.

"It's nothing to worry about." I turned to Nolan. "He's a friend of our pack, trusted by my father, and welcomed here."

His brows touched his hairline. "But how? He's a demon." He looked in the direction Skye had gone. "She seems very concerned about him."

Jealous, much?

"We've been friends since we were kids," I explained. "And she is concerned about him. He saved Skye's life when she was a child. He was only a boy himself at the time. After that, he was raised right here within our pack. We've all grown up together."

"How did he save her, and from what?"

I inhaled deeply as I recalled that memory. "She wandered off into the forest one night and was attacked by a Bleeder." I nodded. "He saved her and earned his place among us."

His eyes widened. "Yes, in that case, he has. But this is still unheard of, a demon allowed on pack territory." He shook his head with bewilderment. "However, I can see why the Blackmoon Pack is so respected. Sadly, I won't be able to attend the gathering since we already know you're not mated to me." He moved to walk away.

I placed my hand on his arm and stopped him. "I'm sorry, but what gathering are you talking about? We won't be having a gathering or a party any time soon."

He stared at me with confusion for a moment, then a look of realization appeared on his face. "I think maybe you need to speak to your father."

I released his arm. "Nolan, please, what are you talking about?"

"Your father has sent invitations to every pack in the area

that a gathering will be happening here within a few moons . . . a gathering for you to find your mate."

My heart clenched. I couldn't believe my father would go to these lengths just to get rid of me. I bit down on my lip, trying to think of a way out. Then I saw a look of pity appear on Noland's face. I was the firstborn of an Alpha—no one was allowed to feel sorry for me, except me. I quickly pasted a bland smile on my face, hoping he wouldn't be able to tell how I really felt. "Alright then, well, I think you should still come. I mean, it will be a party, after all." When he gave me a tight-lipped smile, I added, "I think I should go looking for those two. I'll see you later, okay?"

He nodded and turned to walk away.

Once I was alone, I closed my eyes and swallowed hard as rage began to turn my vision red.

7

―――――

SKYE

It didn't take long for me to find Cyrus. Other than our favorite spot close to the pack, there was another place Cyrus and I often went—the spot where we'd met so many years ago.

I placed my hand on my shoulder, where the scar from that day remained. I'd always been curious—usually a little too curious. As a child, I had never stopped asking questions and loved to explore. On the night I met Cyrus, I had seen a large bird fly over my house and had gone into the forest to investigate.

At seven years old, I had yet to experience my first change. In the pack, children who hadn't shifted yet were carefully watched, so I had to plan carefully. I'd waited until everyone was asleep, then snuck out to hunt the strange bird. Only, at the time, I had no idea I would be the one being hunted.

The vampire came out of nowhere, throwing me towards a tree. I was knocked out for a few seconds from the impact of my back hitting the tree's trunk, and my shoulder burned with pain where the vampire grabbed me. Its nails pierced my flesh, but it was its eyes that I still dreamt of, even now.

Back then, the vampire species was even more reclusive than they were now. If anyone came across a vampire at that time, they usually didn't live to tell the tale. It had become a bit more common to see Skins—vampires who could pass as human in behavior and appearance—in recent years. But it was still rare to come across the Skins' blood-crazy and hideous counterparts, the Bleeders. They were the ones who lacked control and would kill anything in their path.

Vampires were the werewolves' biggest enemy. We specialized in protecting others, both humans and supernaturals, while vampires slaughtered and fed on everything that had blood within its veins.

What attacked me was a Bleeder. The gray-skinned, hairless creature didn't see a scared child. All it saw was food.

My eyes cracked open the moment it rushed at me, its eyes wide with hunger. Then, suddenly, something tore into it. The vampire flew backward, crashing into a tree and breaking it in half.

Through my pain, I saw red wings attached to a boy with bright gray eyes before the world around me fell into darkness. When I woke up, I was back home, tight bandages wrapped around my stomach, back, and left shoulder.

I felt relieved to be home and safe, but I worried about the little boy who had risked his life to help me. It hadn't been a bird I had seen at all, but him. I had no idea what he was back then. All I knew was that I needed to know if he was okay as well.

He had walked into my room as I was trying to get out of bed and immediately called for my mother. I couldn't take my eyes off the dirty boy with ripped clothes. But none of that had mattered to me. I couldn't look away from his sad eyes.

My mother rushed in, tears of happiness running down her face that I had finally woken up after two days. She was hugging Cyrus just as Elinor and Alpha Grayson had walked in.

"I saw your wings. What are you?" I had asked Cyrus.

He looked at our Alpha and mumbled, "I am a demon, and I know I can't stay."

"Were you the one who saved me?" I inquired.

He smiled weakly and replied, "Yes."

I simply couldn't believe it. Seeing him up close, he was even smaller than I was and incredibly thin. How had he managed to kill a vampire on his own?

Alpha Grayson did what I hadn't fully understood back then, something I now knew to be the noblest thing I'd ever seen. "For saving the life of our Skye, the pack owes you a debt. For that reason, you're welcome to stay with us, child, for as long as you wish."

"You're so thin. Do you eat normal food?" my mother had asked him.

As he'd nodded yes, his long tangled black hair fell into his face. Cyrus had shocked us all—even Elinor and me—when he ran towards my mother and hugged her as he wept. From that day on, he lived with my mother and me. Since my mother was mateless and had borne me out of wedlock, Cyrus quickly grew into the role of the man of the house.

Cyrus would go away from time to time, sometimes for long periods, but he always returned. Over time, we learned about his history—and what kind of demon he was precisely

—but it didn't matter. My mother accepted him, and the rest of the pack did as well.

I stopped walking as I spotted him lying under the tree where he'd saved me back then.

His chest rose and fell as he sighed loudly and sat up. "You shouldn't have come." He pinned me with his bright eyes.

I only shook my head as I sat down beside him. "If you thought I wouldn't come looking for you, you don't know me very well." I rested my head back against the tree and gazed up at the starry sky.

We didn't speak for a long time as we both sat in silence, happy for each other's company.

"Do you want to talk about it?" I inquired after a while, my eyes still focused on the stars.

He didn't say anything.

I didn't know if he would answer at all, but I waited.

"I had to attend a ball hosted by my father."

I blinked rapidly. He'd never spoken about his father before, so this I found interesting. "Oh," I replied simply. "How did that go?"

"My father is the Demon King, Skye—the Lord of the Underworld. I'm just one of his many children. Honestly, I thought he wouldn't even know who I was . . ." He shook his head. "He did."

I swallowed, not sure what to do with this information. Cyrus was the son of the Demon King. *The* Demon King? Now I understood why he'd kept that information to himself. He was literally a prince of Hell. "Wow, um," I mumbled. "So, what happened?"

He didn't say anything just then. Instead, he stared at me intently, his eyes darting back and forth over my face. "Never let my heritage change how you see me. I'm nothing like him."

I narrowed my eyes—and then I couldn't stop myself from laughing.

He looked at me with concern as my laughter echoed around us.

"Oh, please." I chuckled. "Why would that change how I see you?"

His lips curved with a small smile. "Good." He crossed his arms over his chest and rested his head against the tree as if he was tired.

"Have you fed?" I demanded. Even in the dark, I could see how pale he was. He'd always get pale when he went too long without feeding. "You didn't, did you?"

His jaws visibly clenched. "That doesn't matter," he mumbled.

I repositioned my body in order to face him directly. I knew he was touchy about this subject, but I couldn't let him get ill. I felt sure he was the only incubus who held back from feeding. Sexual energy was fuel for him. While I didn't want to think about him having sex with someone, I didn't want him to get sick, either. "Are you kidding? You're already pale, and you know what comes next. Why didn't you feed when you went home?"

"Let it go, Skye, okay? I'm not hungry. I wasn't then, and I'm not now."

I ignored the edge in his voice. "Is that why you flew off like that back there, why you're so on edge?"

He merely continued to peer up at the sky.

I grew furious. "I hate it when you do that. Stop ignoring my questions."

"Trust me for once that I'm okay." His head tilted to the side, and he smiled at me, acting like the Cyrus I knew and loved. "I'm just glad I got back okay. You worry too much."

I didn't buy it. "I wouldn't worry if you'd stop starving yourself," I argued. "You can literally feed on anyone—human or supernatural—and yet, you refuse. Feed on me, then!"

His face fell. His pupils expanded for a moment, almost turning all the gray of his eyes black before turning to normal. "That's not funny, Skye, and you know it."

"Does it look like I'm joking? You need to feed, and I don't mind helping you."

He shook his head and got up. "That wouldn't help, trust me. I could never feed on you."

I got up as well, brushing my hand down my dress. "Why not?"

He started to walk away.

I ran forward and stopped in front of him. He moved to the left, and so did I. When he moved to the right, I blocked him again. "Why not?"

His arms shot out suddenly and grabbed my shoulders. "Because I don't know if I'd be able to stop, okay!" His rigid shoulders relaxed. "You don't know what it's like. I could go too far."

Something about his words had my stomach clenching. Why was his denial making me even more curious to know what it felt like? To be honest, I'd heard people talk about their experiences with sex demons, of the thrill and freedom they'd felt. Despite acting a little boy-crazy now and then, I'd never dated anyone seriously. "Oh," was all I could say. "I understand."

His hands fell away from my shoulders. "Good." He reached out and took one of my curls, stretching it, then grinned as it bounced back into place. His smile was short-lived, however. "My mother said something to me while I was down there, something I can't stop thinking about." His eyes moved from my hair to my face. "She said the werewolves I loved so much wouldn't be around for much longer."

I frowned. "Well, that's dark. But when you think about it, demons do live longer than most supernaturals. Maybe she was just trying to get a reaction out of you." I shrugged. "At this point, I think she'll say anything to scare you into leaving us."

He looked thoughtful for a moment as he pushed his hand through his hair. Still, a few strands fell into his face. His hair had grown so much in such a short time.

Then again, I remembered just how different time was in the Underworld. "How long were you there for?"

He puckered his mouth thoughtfully. "Almost two weeks."

My eyes widened. "Wow, okay then. So what happened with your father? Are you his successor? Am I hanging out with the next Demon King?"

He roared with laughter, a genuine laugh this time.

I breathed a sigh of relief. My light-hearted Cyrus was returning.

"Hell, no!" He chuckled low. "He has many, many children, and only the ones born to the Queen can be successors. But I do have my mother to worry about. She's after me to take over our clan."

"If you do that, you won't be able to stay on Earth, right?" I probed. But I already knew the answer. He'd become Lust—a Sin. Of course he wouldn't be able to spend much time here! He would be too busy doing whatever it was Sins did.

He nodded. "Yeah." He reached out and pinched my chin before playfully shaking my head from side to side. "But I can't see myself leaving you." He glanced away quickly, releasing me. "Elinor as well, of course." He cleared his throat.

"Yes," I whispered. "Elinor as well."

Was there something between us, something other than friendship? Nope. There had never been, but after years of living with him, years of looking up to him . . . even with him acting as my protector, I did like him as more than just a friend.

Still, no matter how much I might wish otherwise, Cyrus was a demon. Nothing could ever happen between us, and I was fairly certain he thought of me as a sister. "So, what else happened? Come on, give details."

He bit down on his lip, then looked away. "I saw someone I had forgotten." His frown deepened. "The only sibling I was able to tolerate before I left the Demon Realm. He's not usually there during my visits, so I haven't run into him in a while."

I felt relieved to know there was at least one person in his family he had some sort of relationship with. "So, I'm guessing you guys were able to catch up?"

He nodded. "Somewhat." He inhaled and gave me a tight-lipped smile. "At first, I had no idea who he was. I felt horrible, especially since he knew me instantly. We were inseparable as kids . . . mostly because he didn't want to leave me alone down there. Still, he was the only one that made me feel . . . wanted."

"You're definitely wanted here," I reassured him.

His lips curved with a sad smile.

"Cyrus, what's wrong?"

"I have no real role within the pack. I live here, and I'm friends with you and Elinor. But I have no real purpose, no sense of where I'm supposed to go." His sad smile fell away. "To be honest, I think I haven't made it a point to belong because a part of me knows I won't be able to fight my mother forever. Sooner or later, I'll have to take over her Legion—either to keep power myself or to pass it on to someone else. Either way, I can't be here forever."

"There you guys are."

We looked around and saw Elinor speed-walking towards us, her hair blowing behind her like a curtain.

"What happened?" I asked before she reached us. I could see the rage blazing in her eyes from a distance.

Cyrus stepped forward, his face morphing into seriousness. "Are you okay?"

She nodded. "I'm fine, but my father won't be after I kill him."

"What are you talking about?" I asked.

Elinor let out a deep breath that sounded a little too much like a growl. "He's invited all the wolves in the area to a gathering—here! So I can find my mate among the firstborns." She shivered in rage. "Yet he mentioned nothing about this to me. Nothing! I only found out because Nolan just told me." She shook her head and closed her eyes. Her voice broke as she spoke. "Does—he not realize how this looks? It's like I'm being sold, like—like he can't wait to be rid of me."

I pulled her into a hug before she broke down, and she clung to me tightly. We stood there for a moment as her breathing slowed.

Finally, she gently pulled away. "I-I'm going to head home. I need to talk to him tonight." She bit down on her lip. "I'll see you guys tomorrow."

Cyrus placed his hand on her shoulder. "Do you want us to walk with you?"

She looked up at him and shook her head. "It's okay. I'll be okay. Are you doing better?" That was just like Elinor, worrying about others when her life was going to hell.

Cyrus smiled and nodded. "I'm fine."

She gave us another tight-lipped smile and turned away.

My heart was breaking for her. Alpha Grayson did seem to be putting a lot of effort into finding her mate. What was the rush? Once Elinor met her mate, she'd have to leave the pack immediately to begin her transition into Luna.

"I know how she feels, having a life forced on you that you don't want," Cyrus said, more to himself than to me as he watched Elinor's departure.

I sighed and looped my arm through his. "Are you staying at our place? I'm sure Mother would love to see you."

He looked down at me as the side of his mouth tilted upward with a little smile. "Sure."

Elinor

From what I understood, arranged marriages were common for witches. Members of two covens would be promised to each other at birth, with the sole purpose of strengthening their magic. I didn't know the details, but maybe I needed to speak with a witch who'd experienced it to understand how she'd managed to deal with the fact that she had no say in choosing a life partner. Because right now, I was definitely having a hard time with it.

The Goddess made a mate for each werewolf, so no wolf would never be lonely. But not all wolves found their mate . . . and they weren't necessarily lonely or unable to experience true love. In fact, many wolves went through life without a mate. It wasn't even unheard of to see wolves marry someone who wasn't their mate.

However, wolves from noble families like mine faced an immense amount of pressure to find their true mates. It was said that when true mates had offspring, the combined genes of two wolves made solely for each other would guarantee strong children to carry on the bloodline. Werewolves were all about strength and power.

Alpha-born females were rare. Born with the strength of an Alpha but forbidden to assume the title, if an Alpha-born female was mated to an Alpha male, they'd be the ultimate power couple. And that was why so many Alphas wanted their sons to be mated to me.

Far from feeling desirable, I felt as if I was being treated like livestock, paraded around like a prized heifer at a fair.

And I was about to let my father know exactly how I felt about it.

I walked into my father's office without knocking. "When were you going to tell me? Were you waiting until the night of the party?"

My parents were sitting together on the floor by the window, talking happily. But when I walked in, the smiles on their faces quickly faded.

"We were going to tell you," my mother insisted.

I laughed humorlessly, shaking my head. "Do you have any idea how I felt hearing it from someone else?" I looked at my father. "Are you really so eager to get rid of me?"

He got up slowly. "What do you mean, Elinor? I don't want to get rid of you, but I told you, you're of age to be mated—long past it in fact. So to avoid months of searching, all alpha firstborns will be coming to us."

"You know, I wonder if you'll force Jackson to find his mate the way you're forcing me."

My father sighed and held his hand out to my mother, helping her to stand. "Elinor, there are so many girls out there who wish they were in your position. You're a firstborn and female. You have power very few werewolves have— male or female. As a Luna, you will be able to do so much with your influence. Besides, you know the pressure noble girls face to find their mates. That is just the way it is."

"Okay then, Father. How about you let me find my mate on my own? You and every other Alpha were either allowed to find your mates on your own or were lucky enough to find them quickly through arranged meetings. I don't hate visiting other packs as much as I hate this urgency you seem to have for me to be mated. I'm only nineteen years old, Father. I'm still young. Stop broad-casting my availability to everyone as if I'm prime cattle to be sold to the highest bidder!" I wiped at a tear that escaped.

My mother released my father's hand and stepped forward, her eyes misty as well.

No, I was not in the mood for her pity. I knew she would stand by my father's decision, no matter what. "You know, I think you're pushing this because you know I'll never give up my dream of becoming a Guard. You hate the idea, and you know I'd succeed at it. That's what I'd be known for. I'd make a name for myself as something other than Alpha Grayson's precious female firstborn." I shook my head as I held his gaze, watching his eyes darken with each word. "Maybe my mate is an Alpha-born, and he's somewhere out there. Maybe someday I'll even meet him. But neither of you care about what I want right now. I know there is nothing wrong with being a Luna. I know I'd still have influence. But that's not what I want to do. I want to use the strength I have the way a true Alpha would. You understand what it's like, don't you, Father? We have so much power, and I hate that you want me to suppress it."

My face was slick with tears at this point as was my mother's, but my father had long since turned his back on me.

"You don't know how I'm teased," I said softly. "Right now, I am nothing but a firstborn. But I swear to you, by the time I die, I will be remembered for more than just that."

I turned and walked from the room, my fists clenched so tightly, my nails pierced my skin. I relaxed my hands as I dug deep inside myself and woke my wolf. I walked by a few men and women who'd obviously overheard everything I had said, if their sheepish expressions were anything to go by.

I started shifting, uncaring that my dress was ripping to shreds. All I needed now was the freedom that came from running, from feeling the earth beneath my paws and the wind on my face.

I ran into the woods, my throat burning as I held back my howls of agony.

I won't live and die like this. I won't!

My father was treating me like cattle, something to be marched around until the right buyer came along, and I wasn't going to take it lying down. No one cared about how I felt about all of this, not my parents and not the wolves that would be attending this gathering, hungry for the power they could gain through me.

I can't use the power I was born with, but I can offer it to others. What a joke!

8

ELINOR

alking home from the market the next day, the argument I'd had with with parents last night played over and over in my mind. Mother had tasked me with getting a few things in town, but I'd been in such a sulky mood all day that I'd taken my sweet time getting everything she needed and now it was dusk.

Suddenly, I noticed an odor so pungent, it stopped me in my tracks. When I turned around, bright yellow eyes pierced mine.

The creature jumped at me the moment I turned around and jerked the carriage, pulling it violently to the side in the process. The bag in my hand slipped between my fingers as I jumped back to avoid being bitten.

"Stop it, you beast! Or he'll kill us both!" The man driving the carriage pulled on the reins of the two-headed wild dog as if it was a horse. "We're already running behind."

"Are you insane?" I yelled. "That thing almost took a chunk out of me! What kind of moron uses an orthros for his carriage in place of a horse?"

I didn't really care who was in there. Even if it was a Council Member, I had no intention of holding my tongue. Orthroses were wild creatures, unpredictable at best. Not only that, they smelled positively revolting.

The orthros head on the left that hadn't attacked me licked the ear of the one on the right as they both growled at me.

The carriage door suddenly opened.

The man sitting atop the small carriage hissed, "Well, now you've done it."

I frowned, suddenly very curious to know who was inside, but I decided to pick up my goodies from off the ground. Cursing, I turned my back to the carriage and threw my smashed tomatoes into the forest. "Great. Just great."

"Are you hurt, child?"

I froze, a tingling sensation rolling up my spine at both the voice behind me and the fact that the person had called me a child. I turned around.

The carriage door was open, but just enough to show a man sitting inside, his black cloak covering his entire body. With his hood pulled over his head, even his face was hidden.

I grew stiff, on alert as he suddenly got up and stepped out of the carriage. Just then, a new scent hit me.

"Master, we're running—"

"It's fine," the man told the carriage driver. "Do you need help?" he asked me as he bent down to pick up an apple still lying on the ground.

That's when I realized what he was—a vampire. This male was a vampire.

He held the red apple out to me.

I took it hesitantly. "Thank you, but I'm not a child," I corrected him as I dropped it into my bag. I had to look up at him. He was so tall and muscular. Still, I couldn't see his face, only his mouth, and the way it curved with a smirk.

"You are to me," he answered when the orthros barked.

"You travel with that thing to hide your scent, don't you?" I paused. Why was I speaking to this male, this bloodsucker, so casually? I didn't know but considering this was the first time I'd ever met a vampire, I thought it would be best to act as calm as possible. This man was a creature I knew little about—I didn't see a fight between us ending in my favor.

"Yes," he answered slowly.

Something within me stirred at the sound of his rich baritone voice.

"Why are you walking alone? There are creatures in this forest that prowl at night, some strong enough to hurt a lone wolf."

"I can take care of myself, thank you," I replied, irritated that even vampires considered me just a little she-wolf in need of protection. "I live in the forest. Just because I'm a woman, that doesn't mean I'm incapable of protecting myself."

"I never said that," he contended, tilting his head to the side. "I can smell that you're a werewolf—pureblood, at that."

Maybe it was the mention of blood from a vampire that got me on edge. I narrowed my eyes at him, my irritation growing, especially over the fact that I still couldn't see his face.

This man can drain me dry, and I'm worried about what he looks like?

Well, from what Skye had described to me, he didn't look like a Bleeder, with their gray, hairless skin. Still, he was a vampire, a dangerous predator even for werewolves.

"Well, I should be going," I remarked hastily as I turned to leave, suddenly all too aware of the potential danger this mysterious man represented.

"I can smell your fear, but you're in no danger."

I froze as those words left his lips. For some reason, they made me angry. I hated being underestimated or seen as weak. Sure, I was currently on edge—I'd never seen a vampire before—but if it came down to it, I'd fight this man with everything I had. I was no weakling.

I turned to face him.

Red eyes flashed from under his hood, and he lowered his head.

I clenched my fists. "Have you considered that you might be the one in danger? And that smell isn't fear, it's your dogs."

"Looks like I'm going to enjoy this trip after all," he muttered under his breath. Suddenly, he turned away and climbed back into the carriage.

What the hell did that mean?

I watched as it pulled away quickly, the dog/dogs setting off on a run, and sighed.

I thought vampires had a stronger, more pungent scent. Why was his scent barely noticeable to me?

I had just met a vampire, and he'd seemed so utterly . . . normal. Maybe I was just so intrigued by the whole encounter that I had failed to zero in on his body odor.

I'd always heard that vampires were mindless, bloodthirsty creatures, yet this one spoke and came across as a well-educated man. I continued on my way home, my mind replaying the entire encounter. It wasn't likely I'd ever see that vampire again. At least, I hoped not.

Still, I had to admit, the man made my heart flutter, and not with fear.

ELINOR

We sat silently as Skye helped me fix my hair. Three days had passed since I'd confronted my father, but my outburst had been a waste of time. The gathering hadn't been canceled, and the following day, wolves from other packs began arriving for the big night.

To avoid meeting any of them before the gathering, I had to remain at Skye's house. I felt constantly anxious and on edge, panicked that my mate was sure to be among the wolves who had arrived for the party.

Skye had acted as my eyes and ears during the days I'd been trapped inside. From her reports, there were more than twelve firstborns present—those who would become the Alpha for their packs—and twice as many second- and thirdborns.

Now that the dreaded night had actually arrived, I felt thankful for Skye's company as she helped me to get ready. But I was also grateful for the companionable silence between us, as my thoughts ran rampant.

I was certain she could hear my rapidly beating heart, but

I appreciated her lack of conversation. She was very aware of how I felt and knew better than to ask me if I was okay when it was obvious I was not.

My mother had picked out a pale green dress that she'd insisted I wear, saying its color matched my eyes. After a long bath in water infused with lavender, I got dressed.

For my ninth birthday, I was given a gift from The Council—a round decoration that looked like a warrior's shield made of iron. I could see my reflection on the polished surface, so I went over to it and stared at my somewhat contorted reflection.

Skye placed the final white blossom in my hair, finishing the crown of flowers. Then she stepped back to admire her handiwork. Then she sat down on the bed beside me, wordlessly offering her support.

I let out a deep breath and turned to face her. "I don't know if I can do this." I closed my eyes as I pinched the bridge of my nose. "I'm worried that tonight will change everything. If I find my mate and become a Luna, I will have no way to do what I want with my life. I'll be committed to my mate, my Alpha, my pack, and what I want out of life will be left behind."

"That won't happen." Skye pushed a strand of hair that had fallen free and tucked it back into place. "Yes, finding your Alpha will make you feel like your world is complete— at least from what we've been told. But Elinor, you won't change as a person—not really. Well . . . you may have to refrain from straddling thieves in the marketplace, but at least you'll have something better to straddle at home instead." She winked at me and giggled.

I couldn't help laughing with her. This was one of the

many reasons Skye was my best friend. She could always make me laugh, even when things seemed grim.

Skye continued. "You'll be in a position to change the way things are for Lunas."

I thought about it for a moment. "You're right," I murmured after a while.

She grinned. "I know I am. You can implement all the changes you want to see. Because honestly, no one else will."

This much I knew to be true. It would be hard to change years of tradition, but I wouldn't let another girl go through what I was experiencing if I could help it. As a Luna, I couldn't be a Werewolf Guard, but I could work to make sure other female firstborns would be allowed to make their own choices.

I stood up and pinched my cheeks. "If I do meet my mate tonight and eventually start to change, kick my ass and knock some sense into me. Don't hold back."

Skye stood up as well, her rose-red dress hugging her curves. "Trust me, I will." She grinned, then suddenly, her face fell. "I might meet my mate tonight as well . . ."

I puckered my mouth. "You're right. Do you sometimes wonder what he's out there doing? Whoever he is?"

She nodded as she bit down on her lip. "Sometimes . . . but not often. After all, my mother never met her mate, and she's doing just fine. I'm in no rush to find him, and she's not forcing me."

"I wish my parents were like that," I whispered as I walked to the window across the room.

The night was a cold one, but it didn't bother me. If anything, the chilly air was soothing to me. In the distance, I could hear the wolves who now filled the forest, members from my pack, and others. Everyone was talking so loudly, their laughter piercing through the trees.

"Father said he'd send for me once everyone is settled inside." I shook my head. "I'm not really looking forward to making a dramatic entrance."

"I don't know. I kind of like the idea. No matter what happens tonight, this party is for you."

"I guess that's one way of looking at it," I drawled. Then I remembered something. As upset as I had been the other day, I'd still noticed I'd interrupted something when I'd come across Skye and Cyrus talking. "So, what was going on between you and Cyrus the other night? You two seemed very . . . close."

She looked away. "Close? I don't know what you mean." She glanced back at me and shrugged, though her cheeks had turned a bright shade of pink "He was just in a bad mood like you said, on edge from seeing his mother and father."

I held my hand up. "Wait, did you say . . . his father?"

Someone knocked on the door.

"I'll tell you later," she replied under her breath.

My heart started beating like a drum.

Skye and I shared a look, and then she held her hand out to me. When I slid my hand into hers, she gave it a squeeze.

I didn't know what I'd do without her. I only wished Cyrus had been able to attend. Although he was considered a member of our pack, Cyrus was aware that his presence at the party could make other pack members nervous. After all, demons didn't usually attend wolf gatherings.

We stepped outside to find Connor waiting. "You look stunning, ladies. Now let's get going. Everyone is waiting."

"No pressure," I mumbled under my breath as I walked away.

I heard him yelp, no doubt from Skye smacking him. Connor was her cousin, and she had no problem putting him in his place.

In the meantime, I kept walking, lifting my dress so it wouldn't get dirty as we walked to the packhouse. The closer we got, the tighter I held onto my dress, my anxiety rising to epic proportions.

I knew the moment my mate caught a whiff of my scent, it would mean the end of this battle between my parents and me. Wolves found their mates through smell, which was why I had stayed at Skye's. I'd know my mate the moment I smelled or saw him. From what I'd always been told, when a wolf found her mate, it was as if a void in her soul was suddenly filled—an emptiness she never realized she had.

Once a wolf found her mate, the urge to claim her other half became blinding. Both males and females sometimes went into a frenzy, the males more often than the females. A male werewolf would kill anyone who stood between him and his mate.

No wonder I felt so nervous.

We finally got to the packhouse. Connor vanished, leaving Skye and me to make our way inside.

Holding my head high, I entered the house and made my way to where everyone stood. Because of the frequent pack meetings, a large room had been created to fit more than forty people inside. I called on my wolf, needing the added strength and courage to face this evening.

I noticed two men standing just outside the entrance to the room, both wearing pale yellow shirts with a family crest embroidered on their left breast. Their gazes swept over us, and I did a victory dance inwardly—two men down.

If either of these men were my mate, I'd know it and so would they.

My throat caught for a second as I stepped into the room. Silence washed over the area like a wave, and all eyes turned to Skye and me. I kept my face neutral as I scanned the room of people. Men, women, and children were staring at me as if waiting for—something.

A minute ticked by, and then two. Finally, I located my parents . . . and saw the irritation on my father's face. I inhaled as deeply as possible, trying to find a scent that stood out among all the others.

"Do you sense him?" Skye whispered, and I happily shook my head.

"No." I turned back to my father, and I could see the disappointment in his eyes.

I didn't know if his disappointment was for me or the situation. Right now, I didn't care.

He isn't here. My mate isn't here.

Will

Above the dark forest, the sky teemed with tiny balls of energy, their light so bright, yet so far away. There was a time, long ago, when stars were thought to be souls. It was said that after someone died, they'd become a star, shining brightly down on their loved ones for eternity. A nice thought, one meant to lessen the fear of death.

Too bad it wasn't true. I wished I was one of those stars right now. At least I'd be a million miles away, instead of at this coven tending to my mother's business. There was a single bright spot about it, though. It meant I might have a chance to see that pureblood wolf again.

Resting my elbow on the arm of the chair, I rubbed my lips with my finger. My fangs pushed against my gums, aching to descend. I needed to feed, but this feeling was more than hunger for blood.

I could still smell her—that pureblood. Her scent was engraved in my mind, and I wasn't sure if I wanted to feed on her or just see her again.

It wasn't just her scent that I couldn't seem to get out of my head but her voice and face as well. She held a kind of pure beauty I hadn't seen in a long time, and like she'd said, she wasn't a child at all, as I'd rudely called her.

To a vampire like me—someone who'd lived far longer than anyone ever should—sometimes everyone under a hundred years old seemed like a child.

But not only was she not a child, that wolf hadn't feared me the way I'd expected.

Intriguing . . .

She was either fearless . . . or foolish. My kind were seen as savages and unpredictable; yet, she'd stuck around to have a conversation, as brief as it had been. She was strong, I'd sensed that much, but she was also young. It was naïve of her to have spoken to me so casually, even if she had reason to be confident in her power to fight me and win.

If I were any other vampire, she might not have been so lucky. Many Skins considered pureblood wolf's blood to be a delicacy.

I smiled at the memory of her statement that I was the one to be fearful of her. If she only knew what I was capable of, she'd understand why even other vampires feared me.

A piece of wood in the fireplace popped and ember flew, catching my attention. What was I doing? Thinking about a wolf like this wasn't wise by any stretch of the imagination. Werewolf Guards hunted vampires.

Still, she wasn't a guard. That much was clear from the way she'd reacted to me, and no matter what species she was, she'd intrigued me. And something like that hadn't happened in a very long time.

Well, I'd wanted to interface with the locals while I was here. I just hadn't imagined it happening quite that way. Judging by the way our first meeting went, if I saw her again, at least I'd have some entertainment before I left.

"Are you hungry?" I turned to the voice that had spoken and found my host pointing to a thin human girl weeping on the floor. "Or have you fed already?"

"I've already fed, Vivian, but thank you," I lied.

I'd forgotten that she was even in the room. I'd known Vivian for some time, but I'd never been fond of her. For a Skin from such a prestigious coven, it was unsightly how little control she had over the way she fed. She reminded me more of a Bleeder.

Upon arrival, I was given a wing of the house to myself, though that seemed to mean little to Vivian. She insisted on popping in at every available moment to offer her company, which was only making me wish I were staying anywhere but here.

Vivian's father, the leader of this coven, was away on travel, a detail which my mother had failed to mention. This had forced me to stay longer than necessary to avoid making multiple trips. There were things he and I needed to discuss, so for now, I'd tolerate his daughter.

"Are you alright?" Vivian appeared by my chair. She moved her red hair to her left shoulder as she crunched down, and the tail of her red dress billowed around her. "I know this coven is small and nothing compared to your true home, but we hope you'll grow to like here."

"We'll see, won't we?"

Smiling awkwardly, she stood to leave. As she walked out, she grabbed the human by the ankle. There was an audible cracking sound that echoed throughout the room, and the girl wailed.

I had done unspeakable things in the past, things other vampires had cowered at. A sour taste filled my mouth at the sight of Vivian dragging the crying girl around like a lioness dragging a freshly killed gazelle back to her den, and I gritted my teeth. My craving for unnecessary violence wasn't what it once was, and many vampires thought I'd grown weak. But they were wrong.

Vampires lived for decades, centuries and more. We could evolve just like any other species, and I'd evolved past this barbarism.

Shaking my head, I stood up. "I'm leaving," I said, and Vivian froze in the middle of savaging the human's throat.

"Where are you going?" She demanded, her voice rising somewhat, and I glared at her. "S-sorry, forgive me, I only meant I can join you if you wish."

"No," I grumbled. "There is someone I'm going to see, and I intend do it alone. Goodnight, Vivian."

I had a she-wolf to find, and even though I had no intention of revealing myself to her—not yet, anyway—I preferred even just watching her from afar to spending one more moment in Vivian's presence. Even if it had only been for a few moments, I'd been more at ease around that wolf than I felt now around my own kind.

I wasn't sure what that meant, but I intended to find out.

With my vampirically-enhanced speed, it took mere minutes for me to return to where I'd met the she-wolf. It was probably too late for her to be out, but I was so desperate to get away from Vivian, I'd take my chances.

Although the busy road held many scents from those who'd used it, it didn't take me long before I latched onto hers. I stood on the very spot she'd stood earlier and took a deep breath.

It was risky to get any closer to pack territory, but I had to find her again. I had to see her again and learn the reason for this craving, this compulsion to be with her. Did I want her … or just her blood?

Elinor

I took a sip of the contents of my cup and watched the performers at the center of the room—a female and two males re-enacting a famous love story from our history. In it, a she-wolf fell in love with a wolf who wasn't her mate. When she eventually met her mate, she rejected him. He was so overcome with grief that he challenged the male she loved and killed him. It was a dark, sad story, though the performers altered it to be a satire.

It wasn't common for a werewolf to reject their mate, but it did happen. Losing one's mate, whether by rejection or death, was like having a vital organ crushed.

While I remained reserved but watchful, Skye was off being the social butterfly that she was. After realizing I wasn't mated to any of the males present, my father called for the performers, hoping to lessen the awkwardness floating around the room.

I'd been introduced to a few Alphas and their families and enjoyed chatting with them for the most part. My father was able to mask his disappointment to everyone else, but I could see it in his eyes. It also seemed crazy that it didn't feel weird for us to talk and laugh with each other after the argument my father and I'd had. We hadn't spoken to each other since that night, yet here we were, putting on a show.

It wouldn't be tasteful to act as if we were at odds with each other . . . but I just didn't like how fake it made me feel. So, when the opportunity presented itself, I took my drink and moved to the back of the room where I could observe.

A wolf held a torch to his lips and blew, creating a large flame that soared upward to the sky. The flames reminded me of the vampire I'd met, and I lowered my goblet from my lips. Vampires were dead, and their eyes reflected the soullessness of their condition. I'd only seen this vampire's red eyes for a second, but they seemed anything but lifeless. His eyes were filled with . . . emotion. A powerful emotion, though one I couldn't identify. But was something like that even possible for someone of his kind?

"Why are you back here all alone?"

I looked to my right as a man approached me.

He wore a black leather vest over a white cotton shirt

with a low neckline. The smooth dark hairs peeking out from beneath his shirt were the same color as his slicked-back hair. He came to a stop beside me, a warm smile curving his lips. "I'm Mathew Greendale, son of Alpha Vincent from the Silver Pride Pack." He placed his hand over his heart and bowed.

I did the same, entranced by his smile. "Nice to meet you, Mathew. I'm just enjoying watching everyone. It's nice to see everyone getting along like this."

He nodded. "You're right. So many packs here are feuding, but they came together for you." His lips curved with a grin. "Oh, the power you hold."

I laughed. "Riiiiiight. You forget, they came at my father's request, not mine. I think it's the power *he* holds."

"With all due respect to him, they came to see you. Any Alpha with a lick of sense would consider himself lucky to win your hand, mate bond or not."

I hummed my response and looked around the room. I hated this. I was not a prize to be won. In my peripheral vision I could see Mathew still looking at me, so I turned back to him. "So," I drawled, wanting the silence to come to an end. "If you're not the firstborn for your pack, who is?"

His eyes scanned the crowd and he bent forward slightly as he pointed. "See the one with a bald head and gray eyes like mine over there? That's my brother, Seff. The truth is, I tend to avoid social events like these because I'm not a fan of mingling. But he was really looking forward to tonight. He's eager to find his mate, and he hoped you were the one."

It was easy to spot Seff—he definitely stood out. Interestingly, the only thing Seff and Matthew seemed to share in appearance was their eyes. Mathew was taller, with a slim body and friendly appearance, while Seff was bulky with a scar across the bridge of his nose. "Hmm, you said you don't like mingling, yet he's the one that looks uncomfortable," I teased with a chuckle.

Mathew laughed. "Like I said, he was hoping you were his mate. I imagine you've dashed quite a few dreams tonight, my brother's included." Then he exhaled. "You're not enjoying this gathering, are you, Elinor?"

"Is it really that obvious?" I asked him.

He tilted his head to the side, a thoughtful look on his face. "Maybe just a little," he finally answered. "But one might also think you're just not the talkative type. I saw the way your eyes smiled when you first arrived and didn't have a wolf rushing forward to claim you. I've seen that look before."

"You've met another female firstborn?" I turned to face him, intrigued to know more about this girl.

"Her name's Kaitlin, and no, she isn't a firstborn. But her father had a gathering, much smaller than this, for her to find her mate. When she didn't find him there, she wore the same look of relief that you did. She's . . . a friend of mine."

I had a feeling she was more than a friend to him based on his grin, but it seemed I wasn't the only she-wolf who had a problem with the way things were. At the same time, she might've had entirely different reasons for why she didn't want to find her mate—like secretly having a boyfriend.

Thank the Goddess I don't have that *problem.*

Regardless, I felt a bit glad to know I wasn't alone in my indignation. "Is it so bad that I want to be more than just a Luna?"

When he didn't say anything, I looked over at him.

His eyes were surveying the room as if he was looking for someone. Then he turned back to me. "I don't think it is. Unlike my brother, I'm not so eager to meet my mate. But if or when I do meet her, I'd never want her to give up her dreams because of me. I'm happy I'm not in my brother's position. He has to keep up an image of power, and his Luna will have to, as well." He glanced at me. "The sad truth is, the mate bond changes everything. The person means so much to you that losing them can cost you your own life."

I nodded. "It's scary if you think about it. But I don't mind the mate-bond as much as I'm afraid I'll never be able to escape my family expectations that I'll become a Luna." I didn't feel weird admitting my fear to a stranger. Something about Mathew, maybe the sense of calm he projected, made me feel comfortable enough to speak candidly. I had sensed it the first moment we met.

However, I *had* forgotten that others might be listening.

"Why don't you want to be a Luna?" a man interjected, coming over to Mathew and me. His salt and pepper hair was cut so short, he almost appeared to be bald. "It's an honor to be a Luna. You're basically a mother to the entire pack."

He glanced at Mathew and then returned his attention to me. "Pardon my interruption and for listening in on your conversation, I'm here with my nephew, Adeeno." He pointed to a man with red hair tied behind his back. "His father, the Alpha of the Emberwolf Pack, couldn't make it. I can't speak for everyone, but I believe they'd all agree that the Blackmoon Pack is one of the most respected packs around. That's why we're all here."

"Whether you're a firstborn and female or not, you still

hold a lot of power. Being the Luna for another pack won't decrease your strength or worth. Because of you, another pack will be stronger. You're not a prize, Elinor Blackwood. You're a gift."

I hadn't blinked the entire time he spoke. I'd never doubted the Blackmoon Pack's stature among our kind. His words rang with truth in a way that even I could not challenge. I was reasonably confident that what he'd just said in a few minutes was what my father had been trying to tell me all my life.

I tilted my head, the same unsettling sensation I'd felt when I'd seen that witch in the market not long ago, crawled under my skin.

"Attention, everyone!" My father's booming voice echoed through the room.

All eyes turned to him. Silence quickly followed his request.

"Now, you all know a gathering like this is nothing without a duel."

Loud shouts erupted among the males, but by my side, Mathew was quiet.

"I call on my best fighter, appointed leader of the Werewolf Guards for the Blackmoon Pack, Darian Grimmwolf!"

Cheering filled the room from those belonging to my pack as Darian made his way through the crowd to stand at my father's side. My father placed his hand on Darian's shoulder and nodded once. Darian did the same.

I crossed my arms over my chest. No, I didn't like Darian, and yes, it was for the singular and petty reason that he was the Werewolf Guard leader. Each pack had a team of guards and a leader who governed them.

Darian, as you could imagine, was a skilled fighter. He crossed his arms over his broad chest, his brown skin glistening in the lamplight. His curly raven-black hair was short at the sides while the top was long and in dreads down his back. His hazel eyes darted over the crowd before they landed on me. He smirked.

He also made it a point to mess with me every time he saw me, letting me know in every way possible that I didn't belong in the Werewolf Guard.

"Now, who will challenge him?" my father roared. "You?" He pointed to a male. "Or you?" He pointed to another.

I turned away to head to the door. I didn't need to see this.

"Not interested in watching the duel?" Mathew said. "Girls usually aren't."

I narrowed my eyes at the grin on his face.

And here I thought he had the potential to become a friend.

"If you must know, I'm going to clean up before the fun starts." I turned and moved to walk away. "And for the record, I'm not like other girls, Mathew."

"I've noticed," he said with a flirtatious smile as I headed away.

The truth was, watching duels—a friendly but sometimes bloody fight between wolves—often left me on edge. I hadn't watched a duel in a long time for that very reason. I knew that sometimes pack members would randomly duel each other as a way of testing out their skills or just for fun. Unfortunately, I had a lot of trouble standing on the sidelines. I didn't want to watch—I wanted to fight. I wanted to feel the same rush of adrenaline I had experienced when I chased that satyr through the market. The yearning was so strong, it was almost painful.

For tonight, I'd dutifully watch the duel from the sidelines and try to focus on the fact that this evening was still a minor victory in the grand scheme of things. At least I didn't have to say goodbye to everyone I loved tomorrow as I was dragged to my new mate's pack. I'd concentrate on that for now.

ELINOR

Darian won his fight against a secondborn from another pack within five minutes. He then took on another wolf and then another until he was finally beaten by a firstborn.

After the duel, everyone ventured outside to the lamp-lit forest.

Having decided to try to make the most of the rest of the party, I stood to the side next to my mother and brother as more wolves challenged each other to fights. I found myself laughing and cheering—the energy and happiness being shared by everyone was contagious.

Beside me, Jackson was having the time of his life watching the fights, calling out whatever he thought a particular wolf should do to win.

"Why can't it always be like this?"

"Maybe one day, it will be," someone voiced from behind me.

I realized I had spoken out loud. "Oh, hi, Mathew," I said as he walked forward to stand beside me. I turned to my mother, who examined Mathew with curious eyes. "Mother, this is Mathew. He's Alpha Vincent's son, from the Silver Pride Pack."

"It's an honor to meet you, Luna Clarice." He placed his fist over his heart and bowed to her.

"Likewise, Mathew," she replied. "Jackson, say hello."

Jackson glanced at Mathew. "Hello, Mathew," he said dutifully, then quickly turned his attention back to the dueling wolves. The wolves had transformed into their final forms.

Werewolves' bodies could change from our first form—that of a large wolf—to our final form—that of a man and wolf fusion. Our front paws returned to arms, and we stood upright. Not all wolves could achieve this form or hold it for long because it was overly straining on our minds. The primal needs of our wolf moved to the forefront of our minds, right by our conscious human thoughts, so focusing could be difficult.

My mother shook her head at Jackson's lack of interest in anything other than the fight.

"Anyway," I drawled as I smiled wide at Mathew. "Aren't you going to challenge anyone?"

He moved his mouth from side to side. "I might."

A thundering thud echoed around us as one wolf grabbed the other around his waist and slammed him to the ground.

"Winner!" my father yelled.

The wolf who'd won howled.

But I only had eyes for my father—he looked so different when he smiled. There were fine wrinkles beside his eyes, and his cheeks were red from yelling. "Who is next?"

Mathew stepped forward. "I'm next."

"Good! You're Mathew from the Silver Pride Pack, right?"

Mathew nodded. "I am," he said, looking towards his father and brother, as well as the other wolves that had come with him. "I challenge Elinor Blackwood, firstborn of the Blackmoon Pack! I'd like to see what Lady Blackwood is capable of."

While everyone was knocked speechless at Mathew's forwardness, I instantly grew excited—nervous, but excited. I glanced quickly at my father.

His face no longer looked cheerful. His fiery eyes met mine and his jaws clenched. "I'm afraid that won't be possible," he answered tersely.

My heart sank.

Then, the salt-and-pepper haired man who had interrupted my conversation with Mathew earlier stepped forward. "I think she should be allowed to fight. She's a firstborn, after all, and the reason we're all here." The man turned to face me. "Let us see for ourselves if she lives up to the strength of the Blackwood name."

Mumbles of the agreement began to echo through the crowd.

Finally, the frown on my father's face relaxed. He'd obviously realized he had no choice unless he wanted to look like he had no faith in my abilities. "It is up to her," he affirmed, looking my way. "What say you, Elinor? Do you accept Mathew's challenge?"

"I do," I answered without hesitation. "I need a moment to shift." I turned to venture further into the forest, where there were no torches. On my way, I saw Skye wink at me. She knew better than anyone what this meant to me. My stomach was clenching with excitement as I removed my dress and closed my eyes, calling on my wolf.

A few minutes later, now in wolf form, I first bounded, then padded slowly back to where everyone was. As I stepped out of the darkness, I heard Skye's voice cheering, mixed with calls of encouragement from the rest of my pack. Along with those cheers were shocked gasps from other packs. Obviously, my white fur had once again caused a stir.

I stepped into the circle created for the duels and eyed Mathew's wolf. His paws and back were a dark brown and his sides, light brown.

I remained still as his black eyes scanned me. I growled to show him he was wasting time gawking at me.

His head dipped as he growled back. He padded to the right slowly, his head still down. Yet his keen eyes were trained on me, registering my every move.

No one made a sound. Only the fire crackling on the torches and the indrawn breaths of anticipation could be heard.

I blocked out everyone and everything as I focused solely on Mathew. Still, he managed to catch me off guard. He made a swift move to the left, and I moved to the right in reaction, but that was what he'd wanted. He rushed at me to the right, his growls and mine mingling together as we collided.

I instantly grasped that he wasn't holding back—his bites were at full force. I had to move quickly to avoid him latching onto my neck. While fighting, werewolves always went for the throat to deliver a swift death or to trap their prey. It was clear I'd have to put my full strength and effort into this fight in order to defeat him. Actually, I looked forward to the challenge.

Our growls and snarls filled the silent night sky. I yelped as he swiped a massive paw at my leg and slashed me with his claws. My jaw snapped at the side of his face, but he backed away at that very moment. I had to admit, I was surprised at how fast he was, but as our fight continued, I realized he was only fighting hard enough to cause a few wounds, then he'd pull back.

Someone chuckled.

I lost focus for a moment when I turned to see the old male who had insisted on me fighting shaking his head at me. The look in his eyes, as if he was disappointed in my performance, caused rage to bubble up inside me. The moment of distraction cost me. I had taken my eyes off Mathew for too long, and I loudly yelped as I felt his sharp teeth sink into my left hind leg.

I bent around to bite him, my teeth grazing his snout, and he pulled away. I rushed at him but whimpered as pain shot up my leg.

I was a fool to have thought Mathew was kind for dueling me. Instead, here he was, making a fool out of me. I didn't bother to look for my father. I didn't want to see the look on his face. Instead, I kept my eyes on Mathew as his pack erupted in cheers.

I stopped moving, my breathing labored. Mathew's tongue flicked out as he licked my blood from his teeth, and I watched as he began to shift into his final form—a towering body of fur, muscle, and power.

This was the form that drove fear into our enemies. In our final form, the human side of us and the wolf battled for dominance. In this form, a wolf could become an almost unstoppable force.

I bowed my head as my bones started to break. Despite his head start, I shifted quickly enough to finish transforming before he did. Changing into my final form was always fast for me—it was as if it was my natural state. Given the way his eyes had widened momentarily, I could tell he hadn't expected me to be able to shift to final form, much less shift more quickly than he could.

Yeah, bet you didn't see this coming!

I'd heard this form was hard to hold for others, but not for me. A month after I first shifted when I was a child, I'd started training myself to change into my final form in secret. It had been very difficult. My mother had forbidden me to try it until I got older, but I was glad I had practiced on my own in secret. From the whispers that erupted around us, I knew I had surprised more than just Mathew by being able to shift so quickly.

I'd be damned if I allowed Mathew to make a fool out of me.

I remained still, my long hairy arms limp at my side.

Mathew tilted his head, no doubt confused as to why I wasn't moving.

I was waiting . . . waiting for him to make a move. . . . And when he did, I planted my feet into the earth.

The moment he reached out to grab me, his clawed hands just inches away from my face, I bent down, grabbed him around the waist, and lifted him off the ground. We began falling backward, and I slammed his body to the ground, then rolled to the side.

I stood up slowly, my pack now cheering loudly.

Mathew shook his head and stood up. He bared his teeth, then rushed at me again.

I swiftly followed his eyes to see his next move.

Without warning, I rushed forward, meeting him head-on. I could tell he had expected me to remain still. Forced to recalculate his attack, he faltered. I grabbed his throat and stepped behind him smoothly to sink my claws into his back. Simultaneously, my right hand tightened around his windpipe.

He reached out to grab for something, but I howled loudly, my body shaking before I bit down on his neck. One of his legs gave out, and I shook my head wildly, my teeth grazing bone before I released him, letting him fall to the ground.

Holding his neck, he flipped onto his back, his blood soaking the forest floor.

I stepped forward.

"That's enough!" Alpha Vincent yelled.

I turned to him, my mind cloudy with an intense need to dominate. My head fell back as I howled to the sky, the sound long and thundering, no doubt heard for miles around.

All werewolves released a chemical that causes other werewolves to submit, but it was stronger with Alphas because it was meant to control their pack.

My skin warmed as that chemical bloomed within me. But it could be painful for wolves of lesser strength. I stopped howling abruptly when soft whimpers met my ears. I held my head high, staring Alpha Vincent dead in the eye and then turning to my father.

His eyes were wide with shock.

A few wolves had their heads bowed while others seemed to be straining to hold themselves back from doing so—a few firstborn males to be exact.

I turned to Mathew, who was still on the ground, and held my hand out for him to take. He did so, and I pulled him up, the wound on his neck already slowly healing.

"Elinor!" Skye's cry of jubilation echoed through the crowd.

Soon many others were chanting my name.

An unbelievable feeling I had no description for filled me. And to my surprise, when I looked at my father, I found him smiling proudly.

Elinor

After most of the wolves retired for the night, I could finally enjoy some peace and quiet. The evening had turned out better than I had expected. I was both pleased and relieved I hadn't found my mate, and I was even more pleased about the outcome of the fight I'd had with Mathew. It was as if a door had unlocked within me— one I hadn't even known was there.

I'd never used that much dominance before. I hadn't even known I'd had it in me.

Sitting by the window in my room, I watched as an owl flew over the house, its loud screech ringing in my ear as I thought about the night's events. Mathew was okay. His wounds were treated after our fight—he'd already started to heal before the battle was over. But something he'd said still bothered me.

"It took you long enough to react," he had whispered to me.

"What?"

He'd only shaken his head and laughed. "It took you long enough to show your true strength. You were holding back without knowing it."

"So you taunted me on purpose, to get me angry?"

He'd nodded but explained no more as his father had approached us.

"Elinor, you fought well," Alpha Vincent noted. He placed his hand over his heart and bowed.

This gesture of respect, especially coming from the Alpha of another pack, surprised me. I felt very honored. "Thank you," I replied quietly, but my gaze shifted to Seff, Mathew's brother, who stood by his side.

"A promising Luna, indeed," Seff had simply commented. His voice was so deep, it was as if he was growling.

We bowed to each other, and then they left.

I guess all those hours spent watching the Guards train are paying off.

A knock sounded at my door, and my father stepped in.

I immediately tensed up.

He held his hand up. "I'm not here to argue."

"I had no intention of arguing, either. You just—never come to my room," I muttered.

He looked away as he came to a stop by the window. "You fought well tonight." He took a deep breath. "Really well, at that. Where did you learn to do that? Have you been training with someone?"

I shook my head. "No, but I watch the Guards train sometimes."

"Oh . . ." He inhaled deeply. "Well, I'm proud of you."

"Who are you?" I asked quickly.

Swiftly, he turned his head and looked at me with surprise.

"Who are you, and what have you done with my father? He would have been livid about what I did tonight."

He laughed jovially, tiny wrinkles appeared at the corners of his eyes.

How long has it been since we've talked like this?

"But thank you," I said softly.

He gave me a tight-lipped smile. "I've never doubted your strength, Elinor. You are my daughter, after all. Do you remember when you said that I know what it feels like to have strength sizzling inside us, yearning to be let free? You were right. You experienced it tonight, the feeling of invincibility that comes with dominance. It felt intoxicating, didn't it?"

I nodded. It really had. I had wanted everyone to see my strength, to understand I was not to be tested. Indeed, I had felt invincible.

"I see a better life for you as Luna. Being in the Werewolf Guard with that much power will be harder than you think. Other wolves of lesser strength will constantly challenge you."

I exhaled with a sigh. "I understand. I'd have an advantage over them all."

He nodded firmly. "Yes. You'd make a great Alpha, Elinor. I don't doubt that. I never have." He looked away to stare out the window. "But you're also kind and compassionate, traits an Alpha can't afford. You have no idea of the choices I've had to make as Alpha."

"If I were ruthless and cold-hearted, would you let me become Alpha? Or even join the Guard?" I kept staring at him, but as the seconds ticked by and he continued staring out the window, I knew he wasn't going to answer me.

"There are things out there that you don't know or understand, Elinor. Things that, even with your strength, you can't beat. I can't lose my only daughter." He turned from the window to face me.

I saw the sincerity in his eyes.

My father had never been affectionate towards me. Our intense arguments started when I entered my teens and felt the need to question everything. Even when I was young, we'd never really taken time to talk about our feelings.

"I understand. I do." I stood up and walked over to my bed. "And I know there is a lot I've yet to learn. I realize being a Guard is a dangerous job, and you are afraid to lose me. Please try to understand what I am telling you. If you force me to be something I don't want to be, you'll lose me as well. I only get one life, and I don't want to have any regrets when I get old."

His response was quick, "We've all had to give up things we wanted to do."

I blinked at the edge in his voice. I bit down on my lip. I hadn't thought of that. "Okay."

"Let's find some common ground here, okay?" He crossed the room and sat on the bed beside me. "You're nineteen, Elinor, soon to be twenty. It's time for you to find a mate. When you find him, there's a good chance you won't become Luna right away . . . unless he's already taken the role of

Alpha. I'll allow you to try out for the Werewolf Guard if you'll work with me and try to find your mate. If you do find him, I'll try to convince him, whoever he is, to allow you to be a Guard for a year before you turn twenty-one."

I thought my heart stopped beating as I stared at him. Had he really just given me his blessing to try out for the Guards? "I—I don't know what to say. Are you serious?"

He nodded.

I jumped to my feet. "Really? I can join the Guards?"

"Well, I gave you permission to try out. Testing will begin soon, but whether or not you will be accepted is entirely up to you."

Without even thinking about it, I rushed forward and hugged him. When I realized what I was doing, I hugged him tighter.

His arms wrapped around me slowly.

I finally pulled away. "Thank you, thank you so much. You have no idea how much this means to me. I really appreciate you giving me a chance, Father."

"It's the only one you'll get, so make it count."

11

ELINOR

After Father gave me his blessing to try out for the Guards a few weeks ago, it still took two days to convince Connor to help train me. No way would I ask Darian for help, especially since I was fairly certain he would only laugh in my face.

Now there was only a week left before testing would begin and my nervousness was through the roof.

All wolves were going to be subjected to numerous tests that would evaluate our skill and knowledge and while I hadn't gotten the same length of time to prepare as other applicants, even Connor said I'd learned a lot during our time together.

I'd always been a fast learner, so I hoped it would pay off now because I was terrified of failing.

If I passed my test, I'd be able to be in the Guards for at least a year. And I had every intention of convincing my father to extend the time when the year ended.

I hadn't been accepted yet, but I felt hopeful.

It took a lot to exhaust a werewolf, but I was at my limit as I ran back to the packhouse. Connor had been pushing me to the limit over the past few weeks, and it was starting to show. My fighting skill had vastly improved, and my body was a lot stronger from all the rigorous exercise.

It didn't help that Connor insisted I train in a dress the entire time, not the uniform I would wear at the examination. He figured if I learned to fight in uncomfortable clothing, it would work to my benefit. Female guards wore breeches when they were on duty, but what would they do if they were needed while off duty? Connor felt that situation was unlikely, but in his opinion, it was best to be prepared.

Men and women in the Werewolf Guard all wore uniforms spelled by witches. The tight black breeches and long sleeve tops were light and comfortable yet impenetrable to tooth or blade.

Unlike the actual Guards, those of us who would be taking part in the examination would wear a twirling rope up our sleeves. It was meant to identify each wolf by pack. Also, we would be given a ring similar to the one all Guards wore. Once we shifted, our uniforms would liquefy and slip into the ring, which would be hidden under a transformed wolf's skin. After all, a Guard wouldn't want to rip his uniform to shreds each time he transformed.

I came to a stop by the side of my house and bent forward, my hands on my knees, as I tried to catch my breath. Connor had to leave four hours ago since my father needed him. I was left to train by myself, but I didn't mind. Tomorrow would be the day I'd find out if I'd be joining the Werewolf Guards.

I made my way inside and upstairs, my legs growing

weaker the higher I got. It was pretty early, but I wanted to eat, take a bath, and go to bed early. My aching joints would be as good as new tomorrow and ready for whatever the examiners threw my way.

I heard Connor's voice coming from my father's office. "We have no leads as yet."

I stopped walking, my ears perking up with interest.

"This is becoming more of a problem than I'd anticipated. We need to be on alert," my father replied to Connor, the concern in his voice evident.

"I know. Darian is continuing with his investigation, but the last b . . ."

I was just about to walk past when my father noticed me. "Um, hey," he quickly said as I peeped through the slightly opened door. "Come in, Elinor."

"Hi, I just finished with my training," I said as I pushed the door open and stepped inside.

Connor nodded. "Good. Now the most important thing for you to do is get some sleep. You'll have to be up early to begin your journey."

I nodded. "I'm just going to clean up first. Ah, what's becoming a problem? I'm sorry, I couldn't help overhearing."

My father waved his hand dismissively before combing his hair back. He reclined in his chair with a small smile on his lips. "Don't worry about that. What I need you to focus on is tomorrow." He pointed a stern finger at me. "Are you ready?"

"I most definitely am," I affirmed, my voice a little too loud.

He laughed in response. "Good. Tomorrow you'll make the Blackwood name proud. I'm sorry I won't be there."

This was high praise coming from my father, and his words threw me for a moment. Praise from him wasn't something I was used to hearing. My determination solidified, and I nodded my head firmly. "That's okay. Cyrus and Skye will be there with me. I'll be okay."

I turned to leave.

Connor joined me at the door. "Remember to watch your rear, Elinor. That's your biggest weakness. Once someone gets behind you, they almost always get the upper hand. Remember . . . you've got this."

"Thanks, Connor, for everything." I walked away and headed to my room, but I couldn't help feeling like something was wrong. What was my father hiding? I shook my head. I couldn't think about that now. Once I passed the exam tomorrow and became a Guard, he wouldn't have any reason to hide things from me.

Elinor

It took us three hours to get to Ruelen, a large town just north of where I lived in Jack's Creek. Ruelen was also only half a day's walk or ride to the sea, making it an ideal center for trade. Humans and supernaturals from all over the world went there to do business. Even though there was another town closer to the sea, Ruelen was usually busier for a completely unrelated reason—duel betting.

The sport had originated in the town years ago, and the set-up was simple. Supernaturals and humans would duel to the death—or close to it—as greedy onlookers placed bets. In the middle of the town stood a large red brick building available just for this purpose. Beyond its steel double doors was an arena for fighting.

This was my first time in Ruelen. I'd always wanted to visit to watch the duels, but my father wouldn't allow it. Today, though, the arena was being used to conduct the Werewolf Guard examination. A long line of werewolves—all wearing clothes like mine—stood in front of the building's double doors.

I looked down at my arm, showing the colors of the Blackmoon Pack, before checking out the other werewolves and the rainbow of colors on their sleeves. The busy town swarmed with applicants along with their family and friends.

By my side, Skye rubbed her hands together with excitement. "This is amazing," she gushed.

We'd be staying for two nights since the examination would stretch on for two days.

Cyrus carried our bags. "This is nothing. Duel matches are held every weekend. That's when the town really comes alive," Cyrus told her. "It's definitely something to see."

"You've been here before?" Skye probed a little aggressively, pinning him with a glare.

"Of course, I have," Cyrus replied casually as we made our way through the dense crowd. "I can fly wherever I wish to go, remember?"

"Elinor!" My name echoed through the crowd.

I quickly spun around to find Raven, a member of my pack, waving my way. Raven's mother, Liandra, was our pack's midwife. While Nurse Hilary handled all of our injuries and illnesses with her herbal skills, Liandra took care of all the expectant she-wolves.

Raven's black eyes twinkled.

I smiled and waved back.

Beside her were seven other members of our pack, all dressed like me. It seemed as if there were a lot of us trying out this year. While Raven looked happy to see me, I couldn't help but notice how the others turned and walked away.

"Good luck, Raven!" She nodded, then turned away, too.

I was immediately reminded of something my father had said—many wolves would hate the idea of a firstborn, or an Alpha-born in general, joining the Guards. I could understand how some wolves might feel Alpha-borns had an unfair advantage or ulterior motives. Nevertheless, what the other wolves chose to believe about me wasn't my problem. I was joining the Guard to help others, and that was the only thing that mattered to me.

Werewolves, as a rule, were protectors. Blinded by the prestige of the position, many wolves had forgotten about the true purpose and importance of being a Guard. Our Guards were responsible for the safety of the entire pack, not to mention the other humans and supernaturals they served. In my opinion, there could be no higher calling than protecting the innocent from those who would prey upon them.

Beside me, Skye and Cyrus were still bickering about him visiting Ruelen without inviting us, whereas I was just trying to keep my composure as I watched more werewolves join the line to enter the arena.

How many would pass the test and be chosen?

"Hey . . ." Cyrus placed his hand on my shoulder. "You'll do great, okay? We'll be in the stands, cheering you on."

"You've got this, Elinor. You've been training hard, and I know it'll pay off," Skye added. "Cyrus and I are going to find an inn for us, and then we'll come back to the arena."

I inhaled deeply. "Okay. Thanks for being here with me." I turned to join the line of wolves.

Just outside the double doors stood a Centaur—half-horse, half-man. His long blond hair with a few beaded twists cascaded down his back, and he had swords on both flanks. I eyed the gold bracelets around his wrists and the crown-like golden headband across his forehead.

He took the names and pack details of each wolf before letting them inside.

Once I had registered, I slowly made my way through the double doors.

I felt stunned for a moment by the size of the place. It looked so much bigger inside than it had appeared on the outside. The arena was circular, with step line seats overlooking a large sandy pit where all the action happened.

I descended the steep steps down to the fighting pit.

An official-looking woman with a clipboard immediately divided us into two groups—men on the left and women on the right.

"Council Member Levi, a word?" A woman with dusty blond hair and dark skin like Skye's approached a stern-looking man that had been standing in the center of the arena, watching the applicants make their way inside.

His purple and white cloak shielded his entire body, but even so, I caught a glimpse of piercing eyes that appeared almost yellow. I found myself mesmerized by them, unable to look away. He tilted his head as he listened to the woman, her voice so low I was unable to hear what she was saying.

All supernatural groups had their own leadership bodies. For us, it was the Werewolf Council Members who set the rules. There were only four of them—one for Asia, another for Europe, one for Africa and another who looked after both North and South America.

Council Member Levi was in control of the Americas. From the whispers traveling through the applicants, it was odd for him to be present.

Although this was the first time I'd ever seen him, something about his eyes bothered me. It took me a minute to figure it out, but eventually, I realized what it was. There wasn't a drop of kindness in them. It was as if he was utterly without a soul. Inwardly, I shuddered.

The blond woman walked away.

Council Member Levi stepped forward, his dark eyes scanning the group. "Welcome, everyone!" His lips barely parted, but his voice traveled loudly throughout the arena.

Everyone fell silent.

"Welcome, applicants. It's nice to see so many faces, so many *eager* faces. I will keep this as short as possible. For those of you who may not know me, I'm Levi Bluebone, Council Member for North and South America. I'm honored to be here to witness this year's examination process. I know many of you are anxious, so let's get right to it. This year, only one hundred applicants will be accepted."

Whispers erupted from the onlookers in the stands.

He went on, "We're aware that this doesn't seem like much, considering how many of you are here, but we need to make sure we get the absolute best. There will be three tests conducted this year." He walked along the line of applicants. "The first elimination process will involve duels. The women will go first, then the men. This will give us a good indication of strength among the genders. During the second elimination process, women and men will duel each other." He stopped pacing.

Silence reigned in the arena as both applicants and onlookers hung on his every word.

"The third and final examination will be conducted tomorrow, and details will be given then. For today, just focus on doing your best so that you can make it to the third elimination test." He lifted his head, the authority he held showing clearly in his voice. "Werewolves are pillars of civilized society—we're protectors, guardians. We are the only ones who fight for the safety of everyone, not just our own kind. Therefore, I will accept nothing but the best from each and every one of you if you expect to become a Guard." He stopped talking, then took one final look at the applicants before turning away.

The blond woman who had been speaking to him earlier made her way towards the female applicants while a bald man with green eyes walked towards the men.

"Alright then!" the blond woman called out. "You may all call me Noela. If any of you have any questions or need anything, I'm the one to ask." She stopped walking. "Meeka Snowbrook?"

"Here!" A hand with a violet swirl shot upwards, and soon a young woman with freckles, curly honey-colored hair, and hazel eyes stepped forward. She looked way too young to be applying to become a Guard, even younger than I was.

Noela nodded to her. "Good." She then turned to the rest

of us, her gaze moving quickly, and my breath hitched as her eyes landed on me. "You're Elinor Blackwood, yes?"

Shit, what's this about? Did I do something wrong already?

I stepped forward. "I am. Is something wrong?"

She shook her head. "No. You're both Alpha-born. Meeka is the third born of the Willowcreek Pack, and you're the firstborn for the Blackmoon Pack. Therefore, neither of you will be taking part in the first elimination process. You'll automatically move on to the second round."

I looked at Meeka and found her already staring at me curiously. "Why?" I asked, frowning because I could already feel the looks of hatred being sent my way. I didn't really care but standing out wasn't what I'd wanted—at least, not like this. "I can take part in the first elimination process, like everyone else."

"That will be a waste of time," Noela replied. "You're both stronger than most of the women here because of your parentage. You're better suited to duel with a man in the second round, where you will have to work harder to prove yourselves."

"This is why Alpha-borns shouldn't be allowed to join the Werewolf Guard. It isn't fair to the rest of us," a voice in the crowd protested.

I couldn't tell who'd spoken, but many women began nodding in agreement.

"Who said that?" Noela's easy-going demeanor suddenly changed. Her eyes narrowed as she stepped forward. "Who said that?" When no one answered, she slowly clasped her hands behind her back. "Okay, answer me this, then. How many of you would refuse to take an Alpha-born with you on a vampire raid?" She waited for a moment. When no hands came up, she continued, "So, all of you would rather have an Alpha-born, someone with natural strength and power, by your side in a raid. But you think it's okay to reject them when you're trying out for the same job because you feel they have an unfair advantage? That's just jealousy talking. You're thinking more about what is best for you than what is best for the group and for the people we protect. If that is how any of you think, leave this arena now. We don't need wolves with your selfishness. Your priority as a Guard isn't to stand out as the strongest or most powerful—it's to protect lives! We're all equals here with a singular purpose. If you don't feel that way, feel free to go home now, and take your attitude with you."

She turned and walked away.

Meeka and I followed.

I have a feeling I'm really going to like Noela.

She led Meeka and me to the stands to watch. "Both of you have to wait until the first elimination process is completed. Do you need anything?"

"I'm okay," Meeka replied, her voice surprisingly husky.

"I'm fine as well," I answered.

Noela turned back to organize the other applicants.

"So you're a firstborn, huh?" Meeka turned to me, a smile curving her lips. "And a female firstborn at that." The first two she-wolves to duel began to shift, their growls grabbing our attention for a moment. "I think it's great that you're joining the Guards, although I don't understand why. Aren't you meant to be a Luna?"

I wasn't meant to be anything other than who and what I wanted to be. It was just who I needed to be for myself wasn't who my family needed me to be, and that was my whole problem. *Why was I meant to be something that was so incompatible with the role assigned to someone in my birth position?* I sighed. "Trust me, getting here wasn't easy." I shook my head. "But how are you here? I mean, no offense, but you look young."

She chuckled, and her cheeks turned pink. "I'm twenty-one. I just look like I'm seventeen. And it took me a few years to get here. My—" Her smile faltered. "My parents only asked that I turn twenty-one years old first."

We were unable to speak after that as the examination progressed. Soon the women's elimination process came to an end, and we were allowed to take a break before the men's contest began.

During the break, I learned more about Meeka—including the fact that she had met her mate when she was sixteen years old. When he'd rejected her, it had taken her three years to fully recover.

A werewolf rejecting his or her mate was rare, but it happened. Our mates were our other half, and I'd heard it was extremely painful physically and emotionally to be rejected—like having a limb suddenly ripped off. Wolves who had been rejected sometimes even committed suicide. It was hard to even think about, but luckily, it didn't happen very often. Meeka was the first person I'd met who'd been rejected.

I tentatively listened as she explained how she had thought of ending her life. Looking back now, she felt foolish for having contemplated it. But at the time, after meeting someone who invoked so much emotion with her, only to have him reject her . . . well, it had been almost too much to bear.

Over time, she discovered that she found her love of fighting by staying active and helping the Beta in her pack. That's when she decided she wanted to become a Guard. However, her parents insisted she wait until she was twenty-one years old before applying. She suspected they needed to see that she had truly recovered her emotional strength after having her heart broken.

"Hey, Elinor!" Skye's voice rang through the crowd.

I caught sight of her immediately.

She sat perched on Cyrus's shoulders above the crowd, not bothered by the stares she was getting from bystanders. "You've got this!" She gave me a thumbs-up, and Cyrus did, too.

"Who are they?" Meeka asked as I waved back at them.

"Skye and Cyrus. They're my best friends. The rest of my family couldn't make it." I turned back around to watch the men's first round.

Meeka asked, "He's not a werewolf, is he? Cyrus, I mean."

"He's not. He's an incubus, but we've been best friends since we were kids." I glanced at her, trying to gauge her reaction.

All she did was smile before turning her attention back on the arena. "That's pretty cool. You know, I find it funny how werewolves don't mingle with other species—even the Guards, who are always out and among others. I plan on changing that."

In the short time I'd known her, I'd come to respect Meeka's level of determination. I felt happy to have met another woman who was just as ambitious as I was.

It didn't take long for the men's elimination process to come to an end. Before we knew it, the second half of the contest was upon us. As expected, many of the women lost. Those who came out triumphant, fighting and defeating their male opponents, received thundering cheers from the crowd.

There weren't many women in the Werewolf Guard, but those who did make it through earned every ounce of respect they got.

"You know, we're not going to go easy on you, ladies," a voice said.

Meeka and I looked around.

A male applicant leaned towards us, a cunning smirk on his lips. "Especially since you're both Alpha-borns." He glanced at his friends, who were nodding and laughing in agreement.

I somehow managed to resist the compelling urge to smash his face in and turned to watch Meeka's reaction. Something told me she wouldn't take his taunt lying down.

Meeka smirked mischievously as if she knew a little secret they didn't. "I see you're only thinking with one head today because if you were thinking with the other head, you'd know today would not be the day to fuck with me. And tomorrow doesn't look good either. Why don't you run along and play with the other little boys and let the big girls talk, okay?" Her eyes flashed black, and a burst of dominance left her body.

The male taunter's face fell. Though he backed up quickly in reaction to her dominance, his eyes flashed with anger.

Meeka turned her attention back to the fight, pointedly ignoring the nasty looks coming from the taunter and his cronies.

I bumped her arm, and she winked at me, making me chuckle. Skye and Cyrus were definitely going to love her.

I sat forward when she was called next to fight, and Meeka didn't disappoint. Diminutive in stature, her wolf was dark brown with white at the tip of her tail. What she lacked in size, she made up for in impressive speed and strength. Within five minutes, she won her fight, throwing the crowd into a frenzy as they cheered for her. Her opponent never stood a chance

As the elimination process progressed, my anxiety shot through the roof, and by the end of the day, my worst fears came true.

They saved my duel for last.

Noela finally called me forward.

I took a deep breath before making my way towards the center of the arena.

"Now, we have Elinor Blackwood, Alpha-born, and first-born from the Blackwood Pack." Noela pointed towards a man making his way towards us, and the crowd began to roar. He was at least 6'8", heavily muscled, with angry, dark eyes and brown hair. "She'll be dueling Ramsy Nightbane of the Blood Wolves Pack!"

I didn't think it was possible, but with his introduction, the crowd began to cheer even louder. I realized he must be a local.

Great.

Elinor

"Try not to embarrass yourself out there, firstborn," Ramsy growled as he started to shift.

I said nothing in response, refusing to allow him the power to distract me. I started to shift, as the pain from my shoulder and then my knee dislocating brought me down to one knee.

I expected the gasp that echoed from the crowd as I completed my shift, so I didn't let that bother me either. My stark white coat was surely a shock to everyone, including Ramsy, who could only stare at me for a moment. He snapped out of it quickly and rushed at me at top speed.

Our growls echoed through the arena as we battled, nails tearing through fur and teeth sinking into flesh. He was strong—very strong—but I was quicker. Still, my speed wasn't enough to prevent him from causing some serious injuries.

I yelped in pain as he swiped a paw at my face, and I backed away quickly, so his nail only scratched me under the eye. I could see from the way he followed my every move that he didn't miss a trick. Our fight stretched on without either of us gaining the upper hand until he acted like he was going to lunge at me but then dove in the opposite direction. I caught the action just in time, but he used his strength to knock me off my feet.

I saw his jaw coming towards me, aimed directly for my throat, and I tried to get away. He jumped on my back, his jaws sinking into my fur and skin. I yelped loudly as he bit down on the back of my neck, attempting to dominate me and end our fight.

I'll be damned if I lose!

I howled loudly, my body shaking as I pushed onto my back legs and caused us both to fall over. I quickly pulled away from him, tearing the flesh at my neck, but I didn't care. I was pissed.

I called on my final form, my bones once again breaking as I turned into a human and wolf hybrid. I growled low as I widened my stance, my arms hanging limply at my side.

Ramsy shifted as well. His wolf was taller than mine, with twice as much muscle.

From the beginning of the fight, I'd been much too focused on his size advantage. I'd failed to capitalize on my skills and natural-born power, especially my Alpha-dominance. I wanted to win without the influence of a power gifted to me purely from being Alpha-born.

His mouth hung open as he growled loudly, his ears pressed against his head as saliva dripped from his mouth.

I didn't move, waiting patiently for my prey to come to me. My genes weren't the only reason I was strong. I'd worked hard to get here, and I'd be damned if I let Ramsy Nightbane steal my dream from me.

He rushed forward, confident he had me where he wanted me.

I curled the claws on my feet into the earth beneath me. The moment he was within arm's reach, I leaned back slightly, pouring my strength into my arms. I retracted my claws on my right hand so as not to cut myself as I made a fist. The sound of his jaw breaking as I punched him echoed in my ear, and he was thrown back, his head spinning.

The cheering crowd fell silent for a moment with shock. Punching wasn't something a werewolf did. It was too human-like, and in this form, we became more enraged. Our attacks became a little more chaotic since we could use our arms to easily rip our opponents to shreds. In our first form, we focused on attacking vital points, but our attacks were limited. But why limit our skills? In this form, we could fight like humans, making calculated attacks if we were focused enough to balance the human and wolf within us. I decided to use it to my advantage.

Howling with rage, Ramsy rushed forward once more.

I paused, my body trembling with power, but I didn't wait too long before acting. I threw myself forward and grabbed his face, my nails suddenly elongating to pierce his skin. I picked him up. As I slammed him onto the ground, the sound of his bones breaking echoed through the arena.

A deafening silence followed as I growled loudly. When I stopped, the arena was silent, then Skye's cheer cut through. The sound of her voice brought me back to reality—I finally let go of Ramsy's face and stood up.

Hovering above the crowd was Cyrus, his red wings flapping wildly with Skye on his shoulders. She howled loudly, and I matched her with the same vigor.

The crowd erupted, chanting my name loudly.

I did it . . . I did it!

"Elinor Blackwood wins!" Noela yelled. "She moves on to the final elimination process!"

A witch quickly ran forward and fell at Ramsy's side. A glowing orb appeared around his body, and the small wounds on his face began to heal.

I walked over to him as I started to return to my human form. My name was still being chanted as I frowned at the odd sensation of my clothing gliding back onto my body from within my ring. "Will he be okay?" I asked the witch.

She looked up at me, her violet eyes laced with confusion. "A few bones were broken, including three ribs, but he'll be okay," she finally answered.

Ramsy groaned. "What are you doing? They are chanting your name, and you're checking on me." He coughed a little before his eyes cracked open.

"Of course, I want to know if you're okay. You're not my enemy. Even if you are terrible at fighting," I said with a grin.

His eyes opened a little more, and he stared at me for a moment. Then he started to smile, shocking me. "A word of advice, firstborn? Stop holding back."

I frowned. "What do you mean? Do you not see yourself broken in the dirt right now? *I* did that."

He started to laugh. "Okay, don't get cocky. I started this fight knowing I'd be facing a firstborn and gave it everything I had from the start. I even thought I stood a chance at winning because I could see the doubt in your eyes. I could see how much you were overthinking. You're a firstborn, and your strength can only be matched by a few. Remember that always. And no matter how strong your opponent looks, don't show them that you've acknowledged that."

I furrowed my brows. "Why are you telling me this?" I asked.

He merely smiled, and the intimating man I had seen at the beginning of our duel was no more. "You remind me of my younger sister. You're as determined as she is, but neither one of you trusts your abilities," he answered as the orb around him vanished, and the witch stood up. "I like a little attitude and a challenge." He winked at me.

"I've healed just enough of your wounds for you to be moved." The witch looked from Ramsy to me as she quickly assessed the condition of my healing wounds.. "You need to be looked at as well."

Three men came over to carry Ramsy away for further care.

I stood. "Thank you," I said as I watched them take Ramsy away, knowing he was still within werewolf hearing distance. His words echoed in my mind. I was Alpha-born, and I couldn't forget that.

1 2

———

ELINOR

I stared up at the ceiling, at the shadows from outside that were cast there. I sighed and reached up, opening and closing my hand slowly.

My fight with Ramsy yesterday during the second elimination process had been brutal. Although my wounds had already healed, my body still ached from the physical exertion.

The moment Ramsy and I had shifted, the crowd that had been cheering for him had fallen silent. I had tried not to be distracted by it—I knew people in the stands were shocked to see my white coat of fur.

Ramsy hadn't been stunned for long. A mere second had passed where he'd been as surprised as everyone else, and then he had attacked. After our fight, several wolves had approached me, asking the most absurd questions.

"Is it true the Goddess visits you every full moon?"

"Can you speak to the Goddess right now?"

"Can you see her? Is she here with us now?"

The looks on their faces when I told them none of that

was true had been pretty hilarious. I was not connected to the Goddess. Other than being a firstborn, I was just a normal she-wolf. Nothing out of the ordinary had ever happened to me.

It always struck me funny that Enchanteds never got the kind of attention I got, especially since they were the ones known to be connected to the Goddess. They were the ones with true special abilities, but because they couldn't shift, they were treated like a lesser race.

Ione, my pack's young Enchanted, was only fourteen years old and had to deal daily with sly comments made by other werewolves. Within my pack, my father made it clear that no one was to disrespect her, but many still whispered about how she was not a real werewolf because she was unable to shift.

I'd known Ione since she was a baby. From the time she was ten years old and had her first vision, she'd had a rough time bonding with kids her age. As a result, her mother, Nurse Hilary, kept her close.

I simply couldn't understand why anyone would mistreat a child for being different. Ione was special, more so than many of us. In the end, all I could conclude was that such behavior was based on jealousy.

I knew what that felt like. I'd dealt with plenty of jealousy from others because of my fur and for simply being a female firstborn. But what I'd faced was nothing compared to what Ione and other Enchanteds had to survive on a daily basis.

I recalled the vision Ione had, about being aware of a full moon. I'd been so caught up with everything else, I'd completely forgotten about it. One full moon had come and gone while I'd been training with Connor, and nothing had happened.

Maybe there was nothing to worry about after all. Enchanted visions weren't set in stone since the future was always changing, but her words and seeing her like that had frightened me.

My mind wandered back to my fight with Ramsy. He'd been my strongest opponent ever, and yet I hadn't felt an ounce of anger or jealousy coming from him for winning our fight.

Our battle replayed within my mind as if it had only just happened. A burning began behind my eyes. Tears I didn't want to shed were trying to force their way out, but I bit down on my lip to keep them at bay. I rolled onto my side and looked at Skye softly snoring across the room.

I wish my father could have been there to see it.

He would have seen my strength yet again and realized there was nothing to fear if—no when—I became a Guard. I made it through the first day. As my eyes grew heavy, I vowed on my final day, I wouldn't hold anything back. Regrets were the last thing I wanted tomorrow.

Elinor

We were all told to arrive at the arena before dawn. I made my way through town, the chilly night air making me more alert. The thick fog filling the streets and the silence created an eerie atmosphere.

Out of the two hundred applicants, only one hundred and

forty-three were left. From the whispers I'd heard, a lot more applicants than usual had made it to the final elimination process.

After the final duel yesterday, Noela had announced that outsiders would not be allowed to watch the final elimination process. This was unusual. I took it to mean the examiners planned to throw something really tough our way for the final test.

I came to a stop in front of the arena.

Meeka made her way over to me. I noticed Raven and two others from my pack made it through as well. While Raven nodded my way when she saw me, the others just ignored me. I didn't care. Their dislike for me was the least of my troubles.

I noticed Council Member Levi, a mostly silent onlooker yesterday, stood beside Noela at the entrance to the arena. And his eyes—I frowned when I realized he was staring directly at me.

I should have expected his attention to fall on me after what everyone saw yesterday. Still, it bothered me that while my duel with Ramsy was competitive and brutal, everyone's attention had mostly focused on my white fur instead of the duel itself.

"Congratulations on making it to the final elimination process," Noela announced, "You've all proven yourself to be strong contenders. This final test will focus on your individual skill and ability to survive even in the darkest nights when evil creatures walk the lands. Although Guards are usually stationed in pairs during a mission or raid, things can happen." She paused as she looked at each of us. "Make no mistake, you will become separated at some point, and you will have to fight for your survival on your own. This job isn't for the weak or faint of heart." She pointed behind her. "The arena has been spelled and made into a forest. Inside the arena right now, there are dark creatures that were captured for this examination."

A few applicants gasped at this new development.

Noela continued, "This elimination process will determine if you return to your pack dead or alive. Anyone that wishes to walk away is free to do so at this time."

We all stood in silence, staring at each other to see who would quit.

A female with a red swirl going up her arm stepped forward.

Noela nodded at the female. "You did well to make it this far, and I wish you all the best. Thank you for coming forward."

The woman nodded, her eyes teary with disappointment. She moved away, and two males—one with a green swirl on his arm and another with a pink one—joined her.

The rest of us stood in silence, watching them as they were swallowed up by the fog.

"Now," Noela continued. "For those of you remaining, Council Member Levi, myself, and a few others overseeing the tests will be watching from the outside. You will all have to survive the forest and the creatures within it for two hours. If at any point you wish to quit, look up and howl your surrender. You'll be pulled from the test. Are there any questions?"

"Why weren't we told the final elimination process might cost us our lives?" a young man asked.

"That is a valid question," Noela replied. "If this information had been given from the start, many of you standing before me now, despite making it this far, might not have even applied. You were all given months to prepare for this. Trust yourself and survive." She stepped aside to allow us to enter.

We all walked into the arena, now an endless forest thick with trees and fog.

I reached out and touched a leaf. Sure enough, it was real.

"Those witches are something else, aren't they?" a man whispered from behind me.

"So, are we supposed to split up or wait for each other?" one of the girls from my pack asked. "She explained that this was to test our individual skill."

I could hear her heart hammering loudly in her chest. "We don't have to wait," I explained, trying to sound calmer than I actually felt. "They didn't give us any rules, other than we have to survive for two hours. I'm sure the way we handle ourselves in here will tell them everything they need to know."

A few wolves vanished into the forest immediately, but the majority of us hung back.

"Alright," I said, taking a deep breath. "Let's do this." The moment I took my first step forward, a female's piercing scream echoed through the forest.

Around me, a few others had already started to shift into their wolves, but Meeka and I only stepped closer together, on guard.

The most disgusting odor I'd ever smelled suddenly hit my nostrils, making them burn.

"Vampires," Meeka hissed beside me.

I grabbed her arm. "Come on!" We started running, and a few wolves followed our lead.

I could hear the growls and snarls of wolves in battle coupled with the hisses of vampires, and I clenched my fists. This wasn't just a test—this was life and death. The sooner that sunk in for each of us, the better. We could die here tonight if we weren't careful.

Beside me, Meeka began to shift, but I stopped her quickly. "Don't! Don't fully shift just yet! We need to get as far away from here as we can. And we'd make too much noise in our wolf forms. Besides, vampires are harder to fight in our first form." I peered behind me, only to see several panicked faces looking back at me. "Can all of you transform into a final form?" Some nodded, though most shook their heads. "Do a partial shift and move as quickly and quietly as possible."

Suddenly, a vampire dropped from a tree above us and fell onto a male. The vampire ripped into his throat within seconds.

I acted without thinking. My body moved on its own accord as I grabbed the vampire and tackled the scraggly creature to the ground. My hand sank into its chest, my claws piercing its flesh so easily. I used those claws to slit its throat three times in rapid succession before ripping its head from its body.

I got off the lifeless creature and turned to the male it had attacked. He was already dead, his heart silent and his skin pale. I clenched my jaw, a gut-wrenching loss settling within my chest. I didn't know him, but I felt like it had been my fault that he died.

The others were staring at me with wide eyes. Partially

shifted, their fangs and claws were ready to rip and tear into anything that attacked them.

"Let's go," I commanded as the forest echoed with cries and screams.

We ran as fast as we could until the stench of the vampires faded. Finally, we stopped and listened to the forest. Thankfully, we heard nothing but silence.

"Goddess, what kind of test is this?" one of two males with us grumbled.

I exhaled with relief, but it was too soon.

A clay hand shot out of the ground, grabbing one of the males around the ankle. He fell forward.

A golem—an animated human-looking creature made of clay—began to crawl out of the ground.

The other male and female who had been with us took off, leaving Meeka and me behind to take care of the golem.

Meeka rushed forward and used her claw to sever the golem's hand from the male's foot. "Let's go!" she yelled as she pulled him to his feet.

We all ran as fast as we could as more golems started bursting from beneath the earth under our feet.

"How do we kill them?" I yelled to Meeka.

"These are clay golems. They usually have some kind of marking on them that shows where a witch has animated them. We'd have to find the mark and wipe it away." She fell forward, tripping over a golem that had just dug its way out of the ground. "We can't do that right now, but removing their heads should slow them down a bit."

A Golem barreled into me and then tackled Meeka. Abruptly, I realized we were alone—the male who had been running with us had vanished. My face twisted with disgust as the golem's clay body latched itself on to me, trying to pull me into its body. "Get off me!" I clawed at the clay stuck to me and then at the golem's head, removing it easily. I looked around. "Meeka?" I called as I turned in a circle. "Meeka!"

She had vanished without a trace.

Elinor

I exhaled and slumped to the ground before wiping my bloody hand on the grass beneath me. The second vampire I'd killed so far laid on the ground in front of me. He had long since stopped moving, his head lying a few feet away. I wasn't sure how much time had passed since this test began, but I was ready for it to be over. I'd transformed into my final form to defeat the vampire, but I wouldn't be able to hold it much longer.

Three wolves had howled their surrender, their cry echoing through the forest. But despite being exhausted, there was no way in hell I would ever give up. I would fight to the bitter end. There was no turning back.

I'd had no idea it would be like this. We'd all been just thrown in here, with no idea of what to expect. Before I ran into this vampire, I'd been chased by a massive spider. Even now, the memory of its red eyes sent chills down my spine. Well, at least I could say I had much better understanding now of how hard a Guard's job was. While I felt sure it wasn't always like this—hunting or being hunted—it was still brutal.

If I slipped up here, I'd never return home. Yet, knowing

this did nothing to deter me from my dream. These were the creatures lurking in the dark who hurt those too weak to defend themselves. I wanted to do what I could to protect everyone.

I stood up shakily and stepped over the vampire's corpse, slowly shifting back into my human form. I watched for a moment as my uniform slid over my body. At first, it had felt as if bugs were crawling over my skin to feel, but by now I had become numb to the feeling.

My eyes were wide and watchful, my steps slow and precise as I tried to listen to the world around me. I faltered for a second as a gut-wrenching howl pierced the silence.

"Meeka," I said under my breath, running in the direction her howl had come from.

I prayed to the Goddess, fervently hoping Meeka was okay. Her howl hadn't been one of surrender—she was in pain. The pungent odor of vampires hit me, and I started to shift mid-run, my steps faltering as my bones broke and readjusted.

Another howl echoed through the night, and I howled in response.

I'm coming. Hold on. I'm coming.

I emerged in a small clearing.

Meeka was in her final form on one knee, a large chunk of her right arm missing.

Two vampires were standing over her, their fangs bathed in blood.

Meeka's wolf whimpered.

I ran forward without hesitation. One of the vampires blurred from my vision and then reappeared in front of me. In my final form, I towered over the contorted creature's body easily. I grabbed its face and twisted its head as its claws sliced at my arms. I allowed the pain to roll through me, refusing to lose my focus. I bit down on the vampire's throat and ripped its head off.

Then the other vampire jumped on Meeka, knocking her to the ground. I noticed the exhaustion on her face. She was covered in blood, and her right arm looked as if she couldn't move it.

I threw the dead corpse of the vampire I'd killed aside and charged at the vampire wrestling with Meeka. I tackled it with all my body weight, and both of us rolled to the ground. Its putrid scent burned my eyes. For a second, the red eyes of the handsome vampire I'd met not so long ago flashed in my mind, and I briefly lost focus.

He didn't smell like this, did he?

No, his scent had been so faint that within moments, I'd become accustomed to it. I'd been intrigued by him, not repulsed. Would I ever see him again?

I cried out as the vampire's claws sank into my abdomen, pulling me back to reality, and I clawed it across the face in response. Flipping us over, I straddled the creature, pinning it with my weight as I grabbed the top of its mouth with one hand and the lower half with my other hand.

Its deafening shriek of pain didn't stop me from ripping its head clean off.

I fell off its headless body, a snarl escaping my lips as I touched the wound on my shoulder.

Meeka's voice met my ears. "You have amazing reflexes."

I looked around to see she had shifted back into her human form. I shifted and rushed to her side. My eyes darted back and forth over her body. She was riddled with wounds.

"I suppose so," I mumbled in response. "Why aren't you healing?"

She placed her hand on my shoulder, blood still pouring from her right shoulder. "That could have gone worse," she said, patting my shoulder.

My frown deepened. "Why aren't you healing, damn it? You're losing too much . . ." My head tilted to the side as her wounds finally began to heal. I sighed. "Okay, thank the Goddess."

"Don't thank her yet," Meeka replied. Then she began to slowly bend her knee.

Then I saw it.

The breeches on her right leg were ripped, but it was the bite mark and the horrifying black veins spreading from it that had a stone forming in my throat. My hand started to shake as I reached out. "No," I whispered. I looked into her eyes. There was such intense sadness there. "One of them infected you."

She nodded. "I can feel it already changing me."

"Kill her before she turns." I spun around to find Council Member Levi behind me, his eyes scanning the dead vampires before landing on me. "She has only minutes left. Kill her, and you will pass."

"I can't kill her!" I yelled as I got to my feet. "She—she needs help."

"She's no longer a werewolf, Elinor. She's a vampire, an enemy. She's going to become one of them." He pointed to the Bleeder on the ground.

My stomach flipped. "You can't be serious! Call a witch! Amputate her leg before the poison spreads. Do something! I'm not killing her!"

"Elinor . . ."

I looked down at Meeka.

She held her hand up to me. "None of that will work." Her hazel eyes turned red for a moment.

My heart stopped beating, an aching pain I'd never felt before consuming me.

"Do as he says," Meeka pleaded. "Don't let me become one of them. Please! Kill me and become a G-Guard." She twisted to her side and groaned loudly. When she rolled onto her back, her eyes were red. "Please—Elinor, k-kill me."

I got up, my entire body shaking. I looked at Levi, in shock at what was happening.

He just stood there. "Two minutes, Ms. Blackwood. Make a choice, but either way, she dies."

Meeka twisted and turned on the ground, her deformed growls causing my ears to ring.

My heart pounded so loudly in my ears, I couldn't even hear my own thoughts. This wasn't how any of this was meant to go. At this moment—*this* was my true test—and it was one I would fail. Even though I'd only known Meeka for a short time, I couldn't bring myself to take her life.

Levi walked towards my friend.

Tears began to roll down my cheeks in earnest now.

He bent over Meeka.

I closed my eyes and fell to my knees the moment I heard him slit her throat, the sound of her blood choking her causing bile to rise to my mouth.

Meeka was silent now, but I couldn't bring myself to look at her.

Levi came closer to me. "I'm sorry, Ms. Blackwood. I'm afraid you've failed."

13

ELINOR

"**A**re you hungry?"

I glanced up to find my mother studying me with worried eyes. I shook my head.

She tried to hide the disappointment in her eyes. "Even a light snack? You haven't eaten all day, Elinor."

I sighed and nodded, knowing she wouldn't give up until I ate something. The truth was, I'd lost my appetite days ago. Skye, who had stayed for dinner, kept glancing up at me as they ate.

I just wanted her to hurry and finish eating so we could get out of this house and go meet Cyrus.

A few minutes later, my mother returned with a plate containing a slice of pie.

My mouth curved downward with distaste. "Thanks, Mother," I mumbled as I picked up my fork and cut off a small piece of the pie. It tasted quite delicious, making me realize just how hungry I was. But I frowned and pulled away when she reached out to run her hand down my hair.

"I'm sorry about what happened, Elinor. I truly am." Mother said in the same comforting voice she used whenever I'd hurt myself as a pup and would come to her to kiss it and make it all better. Her warm hand came up to cup my cheeks.

I peered up at her concerned face and closed my eyes. "It's okay." I opened my eyes again. "I made a deal with Father, and I will stand by it. So, I guess we'll be visiting another pack soon?"

She nodded and turned away.

I quickly finished the pie, then dragged Skye outside. We didn't talk as we made our way into the forest, but the silence wasn't an awkward one. Cyrus soon joined us. My best friends' comforting presence and understanding were the only things keeping me together.

I dangled my legs over the cliff and sighed. Despite the darkness, I could easily see the rushing river below and the rocks sticking out of it.

It had been seven days since I returned home a failure. Sure, everyone was talking about how well I had done over-all. But in the end, I had still failed. I closed my eyes, and in my mind, I saw Meeka lying there, bleeding out. "Damn it," I mumbled under my breath.

Both Cyrus and Skye looked my way at the same time.

I hadn't spoken much since returning . . . since leaving the arena, to be exact. I had no words to describe what I was feeling. . . . I just felt numb. Of course, by the time Cyrus, Skye, and I made it back to the pack, everyone already knew what had happened.

When I got home, I locked myself in my room for an entire day—mainly to avoid any questions, but also because I just couldn't bear to be around anyone. Even after I came out of my room, I didn't say much to anyone.

Meeka's death had been a horrible tragedy. Her life shouldn't have ended like that. None of the wolves who died should have lost their lives during a test.

A test!

Raven and a male from our pack managed to finish the examination successfully, although both had been in rough shape in the end. I was happy someone was capable of making our pack proud, at least.

They were both lucky they didn't have to face the same choice I did. I hadn't heard of anyone who was asked to kill a fellow wolf in order to become a Guard. And Meeka was a fellow wolf—she hadn't turned, not completely. I knew it was foolish to think like that. She had been turning. It would have only been a matter of time, but I just couldn't. When I looked at her, I saw a victim. I couldn't murder her, even if it was a mercy killing.

"She was strong . . ." The words slipped from my lips suddenly, and I began to tear up.

"You don't have to talk about it," Cyrus whispered. He put his arm over my shoulder to comfort me.

I shook my head. "I need to. I can't let this continue to eat me up. She didn't deserve to die like that. None of them did." I pinched the bridge of my nose as Meeka's sad eyes appeared in my mind. "Levi was so calm while she just laid there, knowing she was about to die. He told me to kill her, so damned casually." I sighed as I looked up at the starry night sky. "I can't see through it. Why did they all have to die?"

"This is just one more reason why I think that our leaders

are heartless beasts," Skye grunted through clenched teeth. She couldn't have said it better. "So, when are you leaving to visit another pack?"

I shrugged. "I don't know. I'm sure my father will tell me. Right now, I'd rather be anywhere but here." I closed my eyes.

Cyrus abruptly stood up, and Skye and I watched as his wings sprouted from his back.

I couldn't help smiling as he ruffled his feathers, but my brows arched in confusion as he began to grow bigger before my very eyes.

His arms elongated, and his shirt began to rip until it fell from his body. His eyes turned black as his wings flapped.

Skye and I covered our eyes from the strong breeze they created.

"When the hell did you learn to do this?" Skye jumped to her feet. "You're . . ." She tilted her head back to look up at him because our friend, who was once 6'2" and slim, was now at least 7' and a mountain of muscle.

I got to my feet slowly, my eyes scanning his body. "I didn't know incubi could transform."

"They can't," he replied.

My eyes widened at the deep bass of his voice. It was as if a new male stood in front of us. Once again, I was hit with the realization that we really didn't know Cyrus. I glanced at Skye.

She held her hands clasped tightly in front of her, her brown eyes twinkling.

Cyrus's eyes drifted to her. "I inherited this power from my father. Being the son of the Demon King does come with a few perks."

"No wonder your mother wants you to take over," Skye said.

He held his hand out to me.

I frowned. "What?"

"Get on my back, just like when we were kids."

For the first time in days, a genuine smile made its way onto my lips. "You're kidding?"

When we were younger, whenever Skye or I were feeling down, Cyrus would fly with us on his back. It had always worked to lift our spirits, but as we all grew older, it had stopped. I could imagine how difficult it would be for him to carry a full-grown adult on his back.

He shook his head. "I'm not. You said you want to get out of here, so let me take you. Even if it's only for a short while."

"So you've been able to do this all this time? You could have carried me last week when we were walking back from the market?" Skye crossed her arms over her chest, but the devilishly handsome smile Cyrus sent her way seemed to soften her instantly. "Whatever."

"Alright, let's go then," I said as he bent down onto one knee. I carefully climbed onto his back and wrapped my arms around his neck.

He stood up and flapped his wings. Cyrus took off on a run and dove off the cliff.

I tightened my hold on him. "Oh my Goddess, slow down!"

He chuckled. "Sorry, I can't hear you."

My scream pierced the night as we fell, the rushing water below coming up to meet us rapidly. His wings extended just before we were going to crash into the water, and we ascended abruptly.

Above us, I could hear Skye cheering us on, but soon I could no longer hear her as Cyrus flew higher into the sky. I sighed as I placed my cheek on the back of his neck, a feeling of freedom washed over me. I hadn't felt this way since the last time we did this as kids.

With the wind in my hair, I envied Cyrus for his ability to fly wherever he wished to go. I looked down at the forest below. I could see the tiny bright lights coming from the houses of my pack members.

Everything looked so small from up here, so insignificant. I exhaled and looked up next, smiling at how close the stars seemed. Holding onto Cyrus's shoulder with only one hand, I reached up with the other, trying to catch one. "Thank you for this," I said.

He glanced over his shoulder at me, his hair blowing wildly. "You and Skye mean everything to me. Nothing is ever too much for the two of you."

I rolled my eyes. "Goddess, don't get sappy on me now."

He dipped suddenly.

I screamed for my life. "Bastard!" I smacked his bare shoulder.

"You started it." He chuckled.

You're with the Goddess now, Meeka. You're at peace.

I exhaled as my eyes slowly closed. I pushed the memory of Meeka's last moments to the back of my mind and pulled forward the good moments we had spent together, no matter how brief.

My eyes popped open as a scream below us met my ears. I stiffened. "Did you hear that?" I asked Cyrus anxiously.

He nodded. "Yes, look below us."

I peeked over his shoulder as I called on my wolf to

enhance my vision. My eyes changed to black and I gritted my teeth as I spotted a frail human running. He had three wraiths hot on his tail.

"Demons," I growled as the man tripped and fell forward.

Cyrus tipped toward the ground, and we descended quickly.

One of the wraiths rushed forward, his body cloaked in black smoke. He phased through the poor man, turning his skin deathly pale.

They're feeding on his fear.

I released Cyrus's shoulder, and his body tensed as I leaned forward.

Knowing what my intentions were, he sighed. "Okay," he said.

I unwrapped my legs from around his waist as he reached around to grab me. Then he threw me forward.

My eyes watered and my vision blurred as the air whipped by me. I fully awakened my wolf, and my dress began to rip from my body as I started to shift mid-air. I howled loudly, alerting the wraiths of my presence.

As they looked up at me, the man tried to run but fell to his knees. No doubt he was exhausted—his energy had slowly been drained by those parasites.

I bypassed my first form and shifted into the final one. This was serious.

No way would I let these creatures kill this man. I might not be a Guard, but I'd never stand by and watch another person get hurt when I could do something about it. The earth beneath my feet cracked as I landed. The force rattled my body, but I still managed to spin around and face the demon, howling with all the strength within me.

The thing's red, beady eyes stared at me for a moment.

I widened my stance and hunched forward. I'd never fought a wraith before, but that would not deter me from trying.

Behind me, a crash sounded as Cyrus landed. He walked forward to stand beside me, his wings flapping once before folding behind him. "I suggest you both leave. But if you wish to die tonight, stay, and we'll gladly grant your wish."

I bared my teeth, saliva dripping from my mouth as I growled.

They turned and vanished before our eyes, bursting into clouds of smoke.

I turned around to find the man we had just saved cowering with fear still, his wide, teary eyes dancing back and forth from Cyrus to me.

"We won't hurt you," Cyrus explained as he stepped forward slowly. "You have our word. But may I please have your cloak? If she changes back now, she'll be naked."

The man stared at him with confusion for a moment, then glanced at me, his eyes rolling up and down my body before nodding and allowing Cyrus to help him up to remove his cloak.

Once covered, I returned to my human form. "Thank you," I told the man with a smile, but he suddenly burst into tears.

Cyrus and I looked at each other.

He wiped at his eyes. "I'm sorry. You just saved my life. Thank you," he said, looking at Cyrus, then at me. "Thank you both. I have three daughters, their mother died years ago, and if I leave them, I fear—"

Cyrus placed his hand on the man's shoulder. "We'll

accompany you home if you wish. Nothing will happen to you or your daughters. Okay?"

The old man nodded, his blue eyes still watery. "What are your names?"

"I'm Elinor, and this is Cyrus," I stuck my hand out of the cloak, but only a little to avoid exposing myself to the old man.

"I'm David," he said, shaking my hand. And as we followed him home, he told us all about his many years as a sailor when he was a young man.

I listened on, intrigued about the places he'd been and the things he'd seen. And while his stories were fun and full of adventure, they also filled me with sadness. All I could do was take comfort in knowing I'd helped to save his life so that he might continue living the kind of life I would never be able to.

Elinor

I pulled the corset around my waist after slipping through my bedroom window.

Outside, Cyrus's wings flapped slowly as he hovered outside.

"I'll have to wash and return this tomorrow. David's daughter was kind enough to loan it to me, but it's really starting to cut off my circulation."

Cyrus's lips curved with a grin. "Well, it was either that or flying home in just a cloak. Imagine how that would look.

But hey, you did say that you wanted to be known for more than just being the firstborn of an Alpha, right?"

"Yeah, yeah, whatever." I leaned out the window. "Thanks for tonight, Cyrus. Really."

"I'm just happy you're talking again."

I nodded. "Yeah, so am I. Well, goodnight then. Are you staying over at Skye's or going off to wherever it is you go?"

"I'm going to stay at her place tonight. I imagine Skye is going to want me to take her for a flight . . . and I'm exhausted."

I laughed at this. Skye was definitely going to ask him to fly with her the moment he stepped through her door. "Alright, good luck then."

He shot upwards and disappeared.

I stared at the piece of the moon peeking out from behind a cloud. It had been days since I'd felt like myself. Confronting those wraiths and saving David had helped me gain some perspective.

I might not be a Guard, but Father never said anything about me not helping others. I just had to find the positive in this situation, to make sure I honored Meeka's memory. Like me, she'd stepped outside of what was expected of an Alpha-born female. And we'd both paid the price.

Elinor

ou've been through worse. Remember that." I stared at myself in the mirror and tried to be convinced by the words that were leaving my

lips. Sighing, I pressed my fingers into my eyes and headed downstairs for a late-night snack.

Tomorrow, I'd be visiting another pack with my father, and I was not excited about it. Still, I'd made a promise, and I needed to stick to it.

Walking softly, I listened to the sound of my bare feet on the wooden floor. After Cyrus took me flying a few days ago, I opened up to my parents about what had happened at the trials, about Meeka.

My mother had cried, while my father's face had only turned red with rage.

Although everyone knew I failed the test because I couldn't kill a werewolf who had turned into a vampire, no one knew of the relationship I'd shared with Meeka. I had broken down while talking to my mother and father. To my utter shock, my father had hugged me so tightly, I thought he might break me in half.

"I'm sorry, Elinor. I had no idea you'd be asked to do something like that," he had told me.

I smiled at the memory as I left my room and made my way through the hall to the stairs. Things between my father and I had improved as well, and he still permitted me to train with Connor. Now I never missed a hunt, either.

"She truly excelled in the tests, sir. She did far better than the other applicants."

I frowned as Darian's voice met my ears, and I stopped walking.

"Sure, being an Alpha-born contributed, but she proved herself to be a leader, an Alpha. She took charge when it was needed. I hate to admit it, but she would've made a great Guard."

Wait a minute, is that Darian speaking highly of me? My lips curved with a wicked smile. I fully intended to rub it in his face, now that I knew what he thought of me.

"It's a shame you had to ask Council Member Levi to fail her. I understand your reasons more than anyone else, but how it all played out wasn't—"

"I know," my father responded.

My body froze, and my mind went numb. *Did Darian just say what I think he did? Did my father arrange for me to fail the examination?*

I reached up and pressed my thumb to my temple. No, that couldn't be. Meeka getting bitten and infected had to have been an accident.

I closed my eyes as a throbbing began in my head, as my thoughts started ricocheting off the walls of my mind. I barged into my father's office, slamming the door against the wall with a bang. "What did you just say?"

They both looked around in shock. It was late, so I'm sure they thought everyone else was asleep. My heart pounded so loudly in my chest I was sure they could hear it. For the first time in days, the sight of Meeka's lifeless body flashed through my mind.

I closed my eyes and shook my head. "You—how?"

My father pushed his chair back, scraping it loudly against the floor as he stood. I saw the regret in his eyes.

"How did you do it? How did you kill Meeka?! You did this!"

"No, Elinor. I didn't know Levi would use Meeka as a means to fail you." He walked towards me.

I stepped back, unable to believe I was looking at my father.

"I . . ." He sighed. "I asked him to fail you, but I never told him how to do it. The method was up to him."

"Goddess, you're a tyrant," I said, shaking my head in utter disbelief. This man—this man couldn't be my father.

His shoulders slumped.

"A werewolf died! Died! You-you listened to me talk about her, you . . ." My face fell as the realization hit me, and I was reminded of his words and the way he had hugged me. It must have been because of the guilt he felt. "I'll never forgive you for this!"

"Elinor—," Darian tried to speak.

I growled at him, my eyes changing to black.

Darian bowed his head.

"Darian, excuse us for a moment. I need to talk—"

I held my hand up to stop my father's words. I didn't want to hear anything he had to say. Not right now—not ever. He had lied to me, tricked me. He had watched me train, day in and day out, with Connor. He had given me his blessing before I left, all while knowing it was for naught. He knew he would get what he wanted in the end.

I turned and ran from the room, attempting to shift while running down the stairs. I choked as the throbbing in my head worsened. I tripped and fell as one of the stairs broke, and I rolled down the rest to the first floor. I'd forgotten there was a full moon, and I was unable to shift.

My claws and fangs were the only things that changed, but I groaned at my foggy thoughts. I couldn't think. All I was feeling was betrayal and rage.

"Elinor!" my father called out. "Don't!"

I got to my feet and bared my teeth at him, something

that would have been seen as a challenge if it had been done by another wolf, but I didn't care. I growled.

Suddenly, Darian and my sleepy-eyed mother appeared on the stairs as well.

"What is going on in this house?" Her eyes fell on me. She saw the rage in my eyes before looking at my father and seeing the regret in his. "Goddess, Grayson, what did you do?"

He ignored her as his eyes turned black.

Beside him, Darian and my mother lowered their heads in submission.

"Do *not* go through that door, Elinor," my father warned. "There is a full moon tonight."

As the Alpha, the amount of dominance my father could emit was staggering. But at this moment, as I strained against it, his power was no match for my rage. I whimpered and growled as I fought against his will, but it felt as if a weight was being pushed onto my body.

I shook my head wildly before lifting my right arm and biting down on it. The shock of the pain gave me a second of relief from the weight of his dominance—and I took that second, running towards the door and kicking it open. As the cool night air hit my face, I took off into the forest.

"Elinor!"

I closed my eyes for a moment as I ran, pushing out all thoughts. I didn't want to think. I didn't want to feel. I just wanted to run. My tears flew behind me as I tore through the forest, and my father's howl followed me.

He would probably come after me himself or send Guards, but I'd be damned if they'd catch me.

I wasn't going home again—ever.

He was not my father, not after this, not after what he'd done. I thought we were making progress, but it was all a game to him. I was just a pawn, being pushed in the direction he wanted for his own gain.

Never had I felt so used, so foolish . . . so heartbroken.

I tripped and fell, wincing as a twig scratched the side of my leg. I remained there on my hand and knees in the dark as I cried.

14

ELINOR

I eventually stopped sobbing, my body too drained to continue. I felt lost, both physically and emotionally.

I had taken a wrong turn at some point and ended up in a part of the forest I wasn't familiar with. I wandered, still barefoot, feeling numb.

Thanks to the full moon, the forest was bathed in a soft glow of light. The world around me looked beautiful, but I couldn't admire it, not when my heart was breaking. I knew my father hadn't planned for me to have to kill someone, but it happened because of his actions, his deception. He had played me, making me believe I was on the road to achieving my dream.

I stopped walking and rubbed at my temples. Meeka would have died anyway, but the choice I was forced to make was to kill her or fail? That was because of my father. And it was unforgivable.

I stepped on a twig and yelped as something pierced my foot. "Damn it." I lifted my leg to examine it when a scent I had hoped to never encounter again made me freeze. My eyes changed to black, and my nails began to elongate as I looked around me slowly. My ears twitched as I tried to listen for the vampire I knew must be lurking in the forest with me.

The words from young Ione's vision that day in the clinic echoed in my head, "Be still on the full moon, or blood will rain onto our land. Be still on the full moon, and death won't follow."

I shuddered, suddenly on high alert. I realized I was at a big disadvantage if I encountered anything dangerous out here during a full moon. For a second, I regretted leaving home. I hadn't been thinking clearly. I'd been so consumed with fury I hadn't cared that I was wandering into the woods at night without the ability to shift.

A twig snapped behind me.

I spun around.

A creature with pale skin made even grayer by the moonlight had tried to sneak up behind me. Before I had time to formulate a plan of action, it lunged forward at me with supernatural speed. Its pale skin was even grayer in the moonlight, and it lunged forward.

I dove to the side.

It slipped past me but moved quickly to grab me once more. Its loud hiss echoed in my ear as we collided.

I screamed as its claws sank into my side.

Its eyes widened as I pushed it away from me, causing it to slam into a tree. It didn't seem to care as it licked its nails, now coated in my blood.

Pressing my hand to my side, I tried to stop the bleeding. My healing process was much slower during a full moon.

I started backing away as it licked its fingers feverishly. I recalled the thin, hideous faces of the vampires that had attacked Meeka. In rapid succession, the short moments we'd shared flashed through my mind, and my rage returned with a vengeance.

I growled and bared my teeth. When the vampire looked my way, its wide, hungry eyes made my stomach turn. It seemed as if it had been so caught up in cleaning my blood from its fingers, it had forgotten I was there.

My hands fell to my side as I went still.

It took one step forward. Its head rose up as it sniffed the air.

I clenched and unclenched my hands as I forced my nails to grow as long as they could. Then I waited for it to make a move.

I didn't have to wait very long. Driven by an insatiable appetite, it charged at me.

I twisted my feet into the earth. Then with a burst forward, I held my clawed fingers together and up to my chest, as if I was holding a sword.

My nails sliced through the side of the Bleeder's neck, causing its head to lull to the side. I acted quickly, severing the head from the body and throwing it into the forest. However, my victory was short-lived.

No sooner had I killed one Bleeder, then another one came running out of the bushes. This one was bigger than the one I had just finished off.

It backhanded me across the face and sent me flying. I grimaced at the taste of my blood as I bit down on my tongue when my back collided with the trunk of a tree.

I crawled onto my hands and knees quickly as it walked

around the dead vampire. Suddenly, I realized the one I had killed was a female. This one was male, his lower half naked, while the dead Bleeder had breasts—small, but breasts nonetheless.

Long, angry hissing met my ears. When I looked up, the new one had his red eyes set on me. I tried to stand, but my leg wouldn't hold me. When I looked down, I saw that a broken branch had impaled my calf. I turned toward the male Bleeder walking toward me, his head shaking wildly as he hissed.

"Can't we just talk about this?" I jested.

In answer, he bared his pointy, discolored fangs at me and rushed towards me.

I gritted my teeth as I pulled myself onto my feet, ignoring the pain that shot up my leg. As I held my hands up in defense, a black blur tackled the vampire. They both vanished into the forest as I stood there, looking around in confusion.

The night became quiet, and I stepped back against the tree. Taking my weight off my wounded leg, I bent down slowly. My eyes still scanned the forest cautiously as I grabbed the branch in my calf and pulled.

I bit down on my lip as my eyes teared up, and I fell forward onto my knees. I sank my claws into the earth, my chest rising and falling rapidly as I pushed myself back against the tree into a sitting position.

It looks like I'll die here tonight. Whatever attacked that Bleeder will surely be back for me.

I could do nothing but sit here and wait for my leg to heal enough for me to run. Trying to move now would attract more Bleeders, not to mention whatever else lurked around in this forest. I sat and gathered my strength in case I was attacked again. Pushing myself would only slow down the healing process.

My head snapped to the side when I heard the noise of someone approaching. I pressed myself against the tree as someone in a black cloak appeared from behind some bushes.

The person stopped walking and stood there for a moment.

I bared my teeth and growled. I might be beaten, but I wasn't dead yet.

A chuckle came from under the cloak's hood. "Brave Little Wolf."

My eyes widened at the familiar voice, and that was when I noticed it—a scent totally unlike that of the vampire I'd left on the forest floor. This was a familiar scent, a safe scent. "You," I growled.

"It's nice to see you again, little one." The man raised his head.

I finally came face-to-face with the same vampire I had met on the road. His scent, his voice—it was him.

Why does he smell different from the others?

He took a step forward.

I growled again.

"Relax. I have no intention of harming you." He reached up and removed his hood.

My mouth slowly closed as his red eyes turned as blue as the sky. I blinked rapidly, confused, but was unable to say anything.

He stepped forward and bent down to look at my leg. As

he moved, strands of black hair came free from his low ponytail to shield his face.

He looked pale like every other vampire, but how could there be warmth in his eyes? How were they blue and not red?

He reached a finger out and touched my wounded leg as he inspected it.

A chill ran along my skin as I hissed. *Who is he?*

He pulled his hand away quickly. "You shouldn't be this deep in the forest," he cautioned, looking up at the sky. "Especially during a full moon."

"I can take care of myself," I snapped back, but it was out of habit. I hated it when a man addressed me as if I was weak and in need of their advice or direction.

He'd just saved my life, though. I knew this for sure. I bit down on my lip.

He slowly looked my way once more as a smile curved his lips. "You can, indeed." His brows pulled together softly, a singular wrinkle appearing on his smooth skin. "But should I have left that Bleeder for you to finish up? You looked like you had it handled." His face became emotionless, his eyes unreadable as he studied me.

I blinked rapidly, not knowing what to do, not understanding why butterflies were doing backflips in my stomach. Finally, I looked away. "Why are your eyes blue? They changed from red to blue. I didn't know vampires could do that. Don't you all have red eyes?"

He cocked his head to the side. A minute went by without him saying anything.

"So?" I probed.

He sighed. "You might say it's a gift."

"So, you're a special vampire?" I smirked. "That's interesting."

"I trust you'll keep it between us." He gently pushed my leg to the side once more with his finger.

I gazed down to see that my wound was almost closed.

Then he stood. "You need to go home now. Can you stand?" His voice sounded like a low rumble, yet it was soothing.

The longer I was around this man, the more I started to question my sanity. Because the longer I looked at him, the more beautiful he was to me.

Clearly, he wasn't like the rest of his kind. Or maybe I was not a good judge of that, since I'd never met another Skin. Still, I couldn't imagine all vampires, Skins to be exact, would be as kind as he was. He'd just saved my life, a not-so-small thing considering he had to fight and kill one of his own in order to do it.

I pulled myself up and put some weight on my leg, testing it. It still hurt—the wound wasn't fully healed yet—but it would have to do. It wasn't like I wanted to hang around here all night, especially when I still wasn't sure of his intentions towards me. I wanted to avoid any more interactions with his red-eyed, blood-crazed buddies if I could help it.

"Good, now go. My kind is hunting tonight and I'd rather not kill any more of them to save you."

I wasn't sure how to feel about that statement.

Don't think too deeply about it.

But—why spare me to begin with? Why not let that Bleeder kill me if he was out hunting with them? Or why not kill me himself? "Why did you save me?" The words were out of my mouth before I could stop them.

Just like before, he stared at me with an odd expression.

Yet, his eyes were so inviting, so normal—I couldn't look away.

He took a step forward, his eyes drifting down to my lips and then to my neck.

My stomach clenched as his lips parted.

Then, suddenly, he vanished. I blinked once, then three more times, in shock. It was as if he hadn't been there at all. I looked around me for a moment, listening to a night bird calling out in the distance before I slowly and quietly made my way back through the forest.

I could feel his eyes on me the whole time. The chill that ran down my arms had goosebumps sprouting on my flesh. It wasn't one of fear but curiosity. I hadn't even asked him his name, but then again, I had a strong feeling he wouldn't have told me anyway.

After what felt like hours of walking, I finally entered my pack's territory. I stopped for a moment and turned around, searching the forest for red or blue eyes, but I saw nothing.

I sighed as howls met my ears, and I turned around to see seven werewolves heading my way.

Will

Through discrete inquires, I'd discovered the identity of the wolf I'd met in the forest. But she was no ordinary wolf. She was Elinor Blackwood, the first-born daughter to Alpha Grayson of the Blackmoon pack. That alone should've quelled any curiosity I had. Instead, it left me with more questions. I knew her lineage, her family position. But *who* was she?

In reality, it didn't matter how I felt about her or how many more questions I had. She was destined to be a Luna, and as a vampire, it was a bad idea to get anywhere near her, especially for someone in my position. I'd stopped visiting the road in the forest where we'd met in hopes of seeing her again. But tonight . . . tonight I'd had no choice but to step out of the shadows and re-enter her life.

And I'd killed my kind in the process.

My boredom and restlessness at the coven house had driven me to take a walk. I hadn't intended to come so close to her pack territory, but somehow, I'd ended up there, as if she'd pulled me to her with invisible strings.

Had I not been there tonight, she would've died.

Bleeders were thoughtless vampires driven only by their bloodlust, but it didn't matter that Skins like me—vampires with control over our feeding habits—sometimes killed them just for being a nuisance. They were still vampires, and my kind did not kill one of our own to save any other species, much less our mortal enemies. If word that I'd killed a Bleeder to save a werewolf ever reached the ears of another vampire, I'd be even more hated than I already was. And I didn't want to even think about my mother's reaction.

For Elinor, my blue eyes probably marked me as different than other vampires in a positive way. To my own kind, they marked me as a freak, though one to be feared and respected nonetheless.

But tonight I'd acted impulsively, my body moving without my control.

Hearing her screams awakened something inside me, a

need to protect that felt completely foreign. In defiance of my kind's typical need for a coven, I'd craved solitude for some time. But a urge to protect another species? That was new . . . and confusing.

Whatever it meant, the need had consumed me, leaving nothing but the impulse to eliminate anyone who dared to threaten Elinor's life.

"What's wrong with you?" I combed my hair back roughly with my fingers as I paced back and forth in my room, the crackling fireplace doing nothing to calm me as it usually would.

I hadn't intended to show her my blue eyes. I'd been too distracted by her wound, too concerned by her being hurt, and I'd forgotten everything else.

Would she tell someone what she had seen? Probably not. If I had to guess, she probably wouldn't want to explain the danger she'd been in and why my assistance had been necessary.

I, myself, was struggling to figure out why I'd done it. No, I knew why, I just wasn't sure how to accept it.

She'd captivated me.

I'd been up close to her wound and the sweet smell of her blood, but I hadn't craved it. My attraction to her wasn't predatory. But that made it even worse.

We were complete opposites, mortal enemies. Not only that, we both had important positions to fulfill among our kind, positions that came with responsibilities we couldn't easily ignore. And if her father or my mother ever found out . . . well, I didn't even want to consider the possible repercussions. It was completely foolish to think of having a relationship with her other than predator and prey. But no amount of logic or self-talk lessened the intensity of the feelings I had for her.

Consequences be damned. Pursuing her was probably the stupidest idea ever, but after tonight, I was done caring.

After tonight, nothing would stop me from seeing her again.

Elinor

My mother picked up the half-eaten bowl of soup she had taken to my room. "Are you sure you don't want me to sleep in here with you tonight? You never get sick, Elinor. I know this has to do with you running off the other night during a full moon. Never do that again. Do you hear me?" My mother never raised her voice. I had obviously truly upset her.

I looked away from the window to stare at her, shocked at the way she was yelling. I couldn't blame her. If our positions had been reversed, I'd have been livid. I could have been killed the other night . . . but I wasn't.

The memory of blue eyes flashed through my mind, and I clenched my fists under my covers.

I had partially told the truth, telling them I had killed the vampire who'd attacked me. That was the truth. Of course, I'd neglected to mention the second Bleeder and the strange vampire with blue eyes. "I'm sorry, okay? But truly, I'm just feeling a little drained, that's all." I pulled my sheet up to my chin. "I just need to rest. I'll be good as new tomorrow. Don't worry."

She hissed with annoyance as she turned away. "All I do is worry. Your recklessness will be the death of me one day." She paused at the door, then glanced over her shoulder. "I hope you know I knew nothing about what your father did. He was wrong." After shooting me a sympathetic look, she walked out the door and shut it behind her.

I sat up in bed, my eyes glued to the door. For a moment, I thought about going after her but decided against it. I knew she was unaware of my father's twisted plans, but going after her to show her I forgave her would prevent me from enacting the rest of my plans for the night.

I pulled my covers back up to my chin and rolled onto my side. I stared out the window, watching as the sunset gave way to night. I laid there and waited, waited until the wee hours when the house and forest were silent.

And that was when I acted.

I threw a dress out my window and shifted into my final form from inside my room. There was no hesitation as I jumped through the window, picked up my dress, and made a dash for the forest. I ran until my legs grew tired and then ran some more, following the path I remembered from the other night, avoiding all the areas I knew a Guard would be.

Vampires hunting so close to the pack was a cause for concern. My father had doubled the number of Guards during the night, just to be safe.

Finally, I returned to the spot of my near-death encounter. I shook my head—I had to be crazy, returning to this place after I was almost killed here. At least tonight I was capable of fully shifting, so if anything jumped out of the bushes, I could deal with it.

I leaned against the tree and waited, waited to get a whiff

of his scent, waited for him to appear in his black cloak . . . but he didn't.

After maybe an hour, I made my way back through the forest, angry with myself for being so foolish.

I had hoped he would return so I could ask him all the questions I'd thought of after meeting him. There was no way could he be a normal vampire, not with those eyes. I loved nothing more than solving a mystery. At least, that's the excuse I told myself.

I was being ridiculous, nonetheless—and reckless, thinking he would return. I just wanted to thank him for saving me.

Even more, I wanted to know his name.

15

ELINOR

I moaned and rolled to my side, the odd sensation of something cool on my skin pulling me from my sleep. I felt it touch my ankle, and I pulled my leg under my sheet. It vanished.

Sighing, I drifted off to sleep once more when I felt the sensation once more, this time across my cheek. I turned onto my back and waved my hand over my face. My eyes cracked open, and my breath hitched as I saw blue eyes peering down at me.

"Come to me."

I bolted upright, my breath catching in my throat as I frantically looked around my room. But I saw nothing but shadows on my walls from the trees outside. I closed my eyes and exhaled through my mouth, my heart hammering inside my chest.

It was just a dream.

I swung my legs over the side of my bed and leaned forward as I covered my face.

He wasn't here.

Both relief and disappointment had me sighing as I got up to pour myself some water. It had been two weeks since I was attacked by a vampire, only to be saved by another. Since then, I hadn't been able to stop dreaming about him.

The blue-eyed vampire.

At times, I'd wondered if I had imagined him. Maybe I killed that second vampire myself. Climbing back into bed, I stayed there, unmoving but unable to go back to sleep. My father was gone on business and had yet to return, which meant my upcoming meeting with an Alpha-born who hadn't been at the gathering was postponed.

He'd never been away from the pack this long before, but I was happy he was gone. We had yet to speak to each other about what had happened. Frankly, I wasn't interested in hearing his side. He was wrong—and we both knew it.

Cyrus stopped by to tell me his brother would be visiting in time to join us at the upcoming festival. Festival Luces was an annual celebration where we honored the start of the Spring season, and it was my favorite event of the year. I needed to think about that right now and not about how angry I was at my father . . . or how intrigued I was by a certain gorgeous vampire.

Cyrus reassured us that although his brother was a handful—most demons were—Cyrus would keep an eye on him so he wouldn't cause trouble. The last thing anyone wanted was for one of Cyrus's relatives to threaten his relationship with our pack.

I wonder if he'll be there.

I shook my head. Why couldn't I stop thinking about that vampire?

But what if he does come?

I groaned as I turned onto my stomach and fluffed my pillow to make it more comfortable. I'd decide what to do when or if I saw him. But for now, I wouldn't worry about it. I hadn't seen him since the night in the forest. Why would he turn up now?

My run-in with the vampires that night had to be what Ione's vision was about. But I hadn't died. My blood had been spilled but barely.

It would have been worse if I hadn't been saved by *him*.

Even if Ione had a long way to go before she had full control of her Enchanted powers, at least her visions seemed to be improving in accuracy.

If I told the others about it now, I'd only be lectured about keeping it to myself and being reckless. It would add one more thing to my father's growing list of reasons why I couldn't be trusted with my own life. If he hadn't betrayed me the way he had, I never would've run off that night. Not that anyone else knew that was the reason.

If anything, this was his fault!

As I fell asleep, I had to admit I kept hoping I'd see the vampire again, even if just for a few minutes.

Even if only to thank him for saving my life.

Elinor

Our small town was alive with music and life. Throughout the town, ribbons of every color hung from every building and post.

Beside me, Skye tapped my shoulder and pointed to the sky.

I gazed upward and my smile widened. Above us, floating balls of neon lights cast by witches filled the air. Since it was almost dark, the lights shone even more brightly.

The glowing orbs moved lower and began slowly drifting through the crowd, offering their stunning light and making the colored strings on every surface glow. A satyr walking past us had his hair painted blue, and in the light from the orbs, he seemed to be glowing.

I grabbed Skye's hand and pulled her through the crowd as I headed to where the music was playing.

Standing on a small stage, a band composed of a guitarist, flutist, and drummer played enthusiastically as a siren sang her song. Her hypnotizing voice called people from all around to see her. Her long blond hair swayed as she moved from side to side, and her piercing brown eyes held me captive.

The smell of food pulled my attention away from her. I glanced at a nearby stall, where a little elf boy turned a roasted pig on a spit.

My stomach growled, even though I'd had dinner before leaving home.

"What do you think he's going to be like?" Skye asked me.

"Who? Cyrus's brother? Well, I don't know. I guess we'll find out soon enough." I had been wondering the same thing ever since he told us his brother would be visiting. In all the years we'd known Cyrus, he'd never introduced us to his family. "Has Cyrus said anything to you about why, after all this time, he's having a relative visit? I mean, I thought he hated all of them."

Skye shrugged. "He mentioned that he'd run into his brother at his father's ball. He hadn't seen him in a long, long time. Normally, he tries to forget where he's from, but I think this is the one family member Cyrus actually misses."

"Well, if he's someone Cyrus trusts enough to invite here, I don't think we'll have anything to worry about." But despite my reassurances to Skye, I couldn't help feeling a little anxious about it. Both incubi and succubi—their female counterparts—were unpredictable, feeding on the sexual needs of both demons and supernaturals. If Cyrus's brother turned out to be trouble, things could get dicey.

The last thing I wanted was a falling out between Cyrus and my father.

Which side would Cyrus take if it came down to it—his brother or us? I shook my head mentally as Skye and I continued our tour of the festival. Of course, he would choose us. We'd been his true family since he was a boy.

Gasps of wonder met my ear, and I turned around to see Cyrus making his way towards us. Only it wasn't Cyrus who had drawn the townspeople's attention—it was the male walking slightly behind him.

Cyrus and the male—who could only be his brother— looked nothing alike. While Cyrus had dark hair, gray eyes, and a body covered in tattoos, his brother's blond hair was loose and fell to his mid-back. His blue eyes glistened under long lashes, and the smirk on his lips told me he knew just how handsome he was. His features were soft, making him a beautiful male, yet he gave off a strong air of masculinity with his staggering height.

His power as an incubus to attract anyone from any species was on full display tonight.

"Hey," Cyrus greeted us as he came to a stop. "This is Theanos." He pointed a finger behind him.

Theanos stepped forward, his eyes traveling up and down my body before turning his sights on Skye.

I narrowed my eyes at him.

The confident smirk on his lips faltered for a moment—he couldn't seem to take his eyes off Skye. "It's a pleasure to finally meet both of you," he told us. "You're even more stunning than I had imagined. Such supple skin . . . and I mean that in the most non-depraved way possible."

Cyrus's eyes narrowed. It looked like Theanos's interest in Skye hadn't gone unnoticed.

"Likewise, Theanos," I answered. "Are you having a good time? Do you like it here so far, or is this not your first time visiting Earth? I know some of your kind has never left the Demon Realm."

He nodded. "That's right, this is my first time." His eyes scanned the crowd around us. "I definitely like it so far." A female centaur caught his attention, and his lips curved in a wicked grin. "Back home, we don't have this much variety of women to—"

Cyrus cleared his throat.

Theanos looked his way. "Um, well, I'm happy to be here. Cyrus has been declining my requests to visit for the longest time."

"Why do you have to make a request instead of just coming on your own?" Skye asked as we all stepped to the side to allow two elves carrying a dead deer to walk by us.

"Cyrus found an unmapped portal when he was a child and mastered traveling through it on his own. That's how he managed to leave the Underworld. Since then, he spelled it so only he can use it. I'm visiting without my mother's knowledge, you see." He pushed his hair back. "She'd lose it if she knew I was here. If I use any of the normal doorways between worlds, a record of it would be stored, and she'd find out."

"I see. So you two are close then?" I probed.

Cyrus rolled his eyes.

Theanos laughed. "Not as much as I'd like. Apparently, I'm annoying to my brother, even though I'm older than him." As Cyrus's face twisted in frustration, Theanos threw his hand over Cyrus's shoulder. "When we were kids, all the incubi and succubi our age loved him, despite the fact that he tried to avoid mingling with them. If anything, it made them even more intrigued by him." He glanced at Cyrus. "He hated that I'd follow him around, trying to act like him. And then he left. I was thrilled to finally see him again at the Demon King's ball."

Cyrus' jaws were clenched so tightly it looked as if his teeth might shatter. "Back then, I got tired of seeing your face everywhere I went. But I admit, I have missed you since," he grumbled.

Theano's head fell back as he laughed.

I got the sense that he enjoyed pushing Cyrus's buttons. *Brothers . . .*

At his laugh, all the women in the area looked his way. Incubi were dangerous indeed, and while Cyrus got the same kind of attention from time to time, he generally kept to himself. I'd seen the hateful looks Cyrus had received from other males because of the interest women showed in him.

"You know what your problem is, Cyrus?" Theanos

quipped. "You're too serious. You need to lighten up, smile a little, and stop sealing away so much of your power."

Cyrus frowned for a moment. The crease that appeared between his brows looked out of place on his flawless skin.

I blinked rapidly as a memory of blue eyes and flawless skin that belonged to someone else flashed in my mind. I shook myself mentally to rid myself of the image.

Theanos leaned towards Skye and me. "Don't let him fool you. This one has a more insatiable thirst than the rest of us Incubi—a byproduct of holding back all the time, I'm sure. Maybe it's because he's spent so much time around you two beautiful women. I mean, look at you."

Cyrus' face turned red.

Skye chuckled. "Is that so?" she coyly asked.

"Oh, yes," Theanos replied, his voice suddenly becoming deeper. "So, I'm the only incubus you ladies have met other than my brother, right? Mmm, I assume Cyrus has never fed on—"

Cyrus gave his brother a push. "Don't finish that statement," he grunted through gritted teeth.

Theanos's cheerful expression changed to surprise. "Oh, don't get upset. I was only saying—"

"Say less." Cyrus turned to face him slowly, his eyes changing from gray to black. "Do not make me regret inviting you here. Stay out of trouble, Theanos. This is my home, and these women are my family."

"I won't bother your friends, Cyrus. Think better of me, will you?" Theanos looked genuinely wounded.

Cyrus's eyes changed back to gray.

"I know these two women are off limits," Theanos added quickly, "But there are plenty more here to choose from. I have no intention of harming any of them . . . but how can a quick bite hurt?" His lips parted with a soft smile, giving a glimpse of extended canines.

Cyrus audibly sighed and turned to us.

"Oh, calm down Cyrus," Skye said. "It's his first time here. Let him have some fun." She pointed a finger at Theanos. "You have to swear not to cause any trouble, though. Our town is a peaceful one."

Theanos nodded. "Of course. As I said, Cyrus and I have a lot in common. That includes not feeding on humans or supernaturals without their consent."

My eyes drifted to someone who was approaching from down the road, a thick cloak pulled over his head. Although the man's face and body were hidden, the resemblance in height to my blue-eyed vampire had my stomach clenching.

A scent I was growing familiar with drifted to my nostrils.

Skye, Cyrus, and Theanos looked up at the same moment as the man walked by us.

Around us, several people stopped to look as well, no doubt picking up on the vampire's scent.

Is it him?

That was all I could think of, while everyone else was probably growing anxious. Seeing a Skin out and about was rare—especially in our town.

Is it him? No, this vampire has a different scent, closer to that of a Bleeder.

"That was strange. I think the last time I saw a vampire here was more than four months ago," Skye whispered when the cloaked vampire had vanished within the crowd. She glanced my way.

Although I could see her looking at me with concern, I was still staring in the direction the vampire had gone. If there was a Skin in town, then maybe *he* was here as well.

It was silly, I knew, but I couldn't stop thinking about him. Why had he saved me? For a few days, I'd gone back to that spot in the forest, hoping he would return and give me an answer. But he never did, so I stopped going. I kept telling myself I only wanted to thank him and discover why he spared my life, but even then, I recognized that wasn't the whole truth. A part of me desperately wanted to see him again.

Why? I didn't know.

"Well, well, well, if it isn't Elinor and crew."

I sighed.

Sure enough, Zenko made his way towards us, his usual mischievous grin on his face. His eyes fell on Theanos.

Theanos's eyes lit up—quite literally—and began to glow blue.

I arched a brow, and Skye and I shared a look.

"Well, who might this fine supernatural specimen be?" Theanos asked.

I tried not to laugh at the bewildered look on Zenko's face. It was the first time I'd seen his signature grin vanish, replaced with an expression of pure discomfort and confusion.

The tone Theanos had used was most definitely a sexual one.

In frustration, Cyrus pinched the bridge of his nose.

It was known that incubi often targeted those of the same sex, but witnessing it was really something to see.

Zenko did a rapid about-face and walked away, glancing quickly behind him to ensure Theanos wasn't following.

Skye's hand flew to her mouth to cover her laughter.

Theanos looked deeply wounded, however. "What? What did I say?"

"Theanos, just don't. People aren't used to that here," Cyrus grumbled, "Just don't feed on anyone tonight, okay? Please."

Theanos only shrugged. "I was only asking. He's not my type, anyway." He looked around, scanning the crowd. "But I make no promises. Still, I should be leaving soon. I need to find where the real party is."

I gasped and stepped back as wings appeared at his back, and a few of the crowd had to duck out of the way to avoid being hit by them.

"What the hell? You have wings too?" Skye exclaimed.

Theanos nodded proudly. Whereas Cyrus's wings had feathers, Theanos's wings had multi-colored scales, like the wings of a butterfly. "My brother Cyrus here isn't the only one in our family with a special sperm donor. My father is from the dragon race—hence the scales."

"Yeah, you're special alright—a special pain in my ass," Cyrus said.

Theanos waved goodbye to us and turned to walk away. Before he took five steps, he was surrounded by women. The dragon race was a very reclusive species—not unlike vampires. But while vampires were reviled, people couldn't seem to get enough of dragons.

"Guys, I'll catch you later. I need to babysit." Cyrus sighed and followed after his brother.

"Cyrus's mother really got around, didn't she?" Skye

mumbled as we watched the women grope at Theanos's wings, much to his delight.

I shook my head as I laughed. "She is literally Lust personified. What did you expect?"

"I wonder if he can transform the same way Cyrus can. That, by the way, was mind-blowing."

I pinned her with a stare. "Are you interested in him?"

"In Theanos? Or Cyrus? Have you completely lost your mind? I'm not interested in either of them." Skye shook her head as she moved away.

I smiled.

Yeah, right. Whatever you say, Skye.

16

ELINOR

The festival attendees peered up at the sky, watching in unusual silence as Theanos spun in a circle high above the crowd. Soon, the wind around him took the form of a small whirlwind, and the crowd below gasped from the lights that suddenly appeared from his wings.

It was hard to look away from the beautiful sight.

He landed on the ground with a thud, and the whirling lights above fell with him, falling among the crowd.

I closed my eyes as a feeling of utter bliss overtook me. It felt like that moment when you begin to wake from a dream, and your body still feels light. I rocked back on my heels as my lips curved with a smile.

Peace. This is what peace feels like.

It wore off after a moment, as it did for everyone else, then everyone erupted into cheers.

Theanos bowed theatrically as everyone surrounded him.

"You can't be a demon with powers like that!" a man told him as he patted Theanos' shoulder.

"I'm only half-demon," Theanos retorted quickly. "I take pride in my dragon heritage, too. I honor both sides of my heritage, to be honest."

I sighed as I glanced down at the wine inside my cup. Music began to play once more, and I looked up to see Theanos and Skye dancing. Behind them, Cyrus danced with an elf, her long white hair swirling around her as she spun in a circle.

A smile curved my lips. Festivals and gatherings of any sort made me feel good. There was just something about everyone being so happy and carefree. Their smiles and laughter filled me with hope for the world I lived in, because sometimes it seemed so very dark.

I couldn't imagine a world where unity like this didn't exist. The truth was, outside of my town, humans and supernaturals didn't normally come together like this.

"Elinor, come on! Dance with us!"

I shook my head at Skye.

She groaned with annoyance. Making her way over to me, she took my cup from me and emptied the contents. "Is this human wine? This won't get you drunk."

"That's the point. I don't want to get drunk tonight."

Pouting, she gave the cup to a man walking past us. He didn't even look confused as to why he was just handed an empty cup and kept walking.

"Why are you so gloomy?" Skye asked. "You love festivals. What's wrong?"

"Nothing is wrong," I told her and smiled genuinely to prove it. "I like watching all of you." I turned her around and placed my chin on her shoulder. "Look at all of them."

We stood there for a moment, watching everyone.

Theanos grabbed Cyrus and began dancing with him. Despite Cyrus's annoyance, they both continued to dance as everyone cheered them on.

Theanos turned out to be a rather fun person. With his perky personality, it was hard to see him as a demon—kind of like Cyrus, although Cyrus wasn't anywhere near as perky.

Skye chuckled as Theanos tried to hold Cyrus around the waist to dip him, the way a man would dip a woman while dancing, but Cyrus grabbed a chunk of his hair and used it to slam Theanos to the ground.

Laughter thundered around us, and I stepped from behind Skye to stand at her side. "Sometimes it's more fun to just observe. Besides, I'm not in the mood to dance tonight." I could see her questioning look from my peripheral vision, but I kept my eyes dead ahead.

"What's been going on with you?" she asked knowingly.

Frowning, I shrugged. "What do you mean?"

"Come on, don't do that, Elinor. I know you. You've been distracted for weeks now. It's like you're not really here." She bit down on her lip. "What happened with Meeka is still bothering you, isn't it?"

"I think about it every day. But no, it's not that. Nothing is wrong. I just think . . ." I sighed. "It's nothing. I'm just in a mood, I suppose. But I'm okay."

She continued to stare at me with concern before exhaling heavily. It seemed like she was letting it go, but I knew my reprieve wouldn't last for long. In a day or so, she'd be hounding me about it again.

"All right, if you say so. I thought your mother was coming to the festival?"

My mouth turned downward. "Yeah, she said she wanted

to take Jackson. They're probably here somewhere." I scanned the crowd, finding it odd that I hadn't run into my mother and brother just yet, when I caught a glimpse of something that made my heart skip a beat.

In the crowd stood a man in a cloak. I swallowed hard as I stared into blue eyes—*his* blue eyes.

He's here. My vampire's here.

I stepped forward to look more closely, but when I blinked, he vanished. I frowned, my eyes darting back and forth through the crowd.

Was it really him, or had I just imagined him?

"Elinor?" Skye placed her hand on my arm. "Are you okay?"

"Oh, yeah, I'm okay. I thought I saw someone." I turned to her and hugged her quickly. "I think I've had too much wine. I'll be right back, okay?"

"Oh, alright then. Do you want me to come with you?"

I shook my head, and she moved away to join Theanos and Cyrus.

Human wine did nothing to intoxicate a werewolf, but it sure did taste good. I glanced in the direction where I had seen the eyes. Seeing nothing, I turned and headed towards the woods to relieve myself. As my bladder grew heavier, I picked up my pace.

I must be losing my mind. First it was the dreams, and now I was seeing him when he wasn't even there. What would it be next?

The further I walked, the more the sounds of the festival faded. Sure, I could've found an outhouse somewhere, but I also wanted a breather. I wasn't entirely sure what was wrong with me, but I was just not in a celebrating mood.

You need to stop thinking about that bloodsucker!

I rolled my eyes at my own thoughts. I'd never had an interest in dating anyone—not that my father would allow it, anyway. Sure, there'd been a few men I'd found attractive, but I'd spent so much time focusing on becoming a Guard, the attraction hadn't had a chance to lead anywhere.

Men also avoided me because of who I was—because of who my father was. As a result, I seldom had much contact with the opposite sex. I didn't understand why thoughts of my vampire made my stomach clench and my heart rate soar. Maybe if I learned his name and shattered the mystery around him, I'd lose interest.

I readjusted my clothes after relieving my bladder, sighing with relief. I spun around at the sound of a branch snapping, my eyes shifting rapidly to black as I called on my wolf. I stood there for a moment, listening and smelling the air, but I couldn't detect anything else out of the ordinary.

My shoulders relaxed somewhat as I headed deeper into the forest. I was just being paranoid.

I didn't imagine him. He was really there.

Finally, I caught a scent, though it was subtle. I turned in a circle slowly, my claws still elongated just in case the vampire I smelled wasn't the one I thought he was. "Come out," I called out as I stopped turning. "I know you're there."

"Good evening, Little Wolf."

I spun around again, a gasp lodging itself in my throat. He stood right behind me! I stared up into those blue eyes, lost.

He smiled.

I did my best to get a hold of myself, exhaling heavily through my nose and feigning annoyance. "Have you been watching me?" I crossed my arms over my chest. "Were you watching me while I peed?"

He snorted.

The human-like action had me arching a brow.

"I wouldn't do such a thing . . . unless you asked me to."

My eyes widened for a second. "That's not funny."

"I wasn't trying to be. There are many things I won't do to you unless you ask me to."

I lost the ability to speak for a moment.

His eyes dipped to my lips before wandering back up to my eyes.

I blinked rapidly and stepped back. I would never admit it to him, but his intimidating aura was a little frightening—and very, very exciting.

He stepped forward. "Are you afraid of me, Elinor? I won't hurt you. I need you to know that." He removed his hood and revealed his face in all its flawless glory. His eyes were burning brightly in the darkness.

As his long, flowing black locks captured my attention momentarily, it took me time to fully process what he said. "How do you know my name?"

He shrugged. "I overheard your friend say it at the festival, although I knew before that. You're quite popular around here, for multiple reasons."

"So, you've been asking around about me?" It was my turn to sport a smug expression, but thinking I could somehow push his buttons turned out to be a waste of time.

He smiled. "I have been. I needed to know about the young wolf brave enough to be out on a full moon. Although, in your case, it was foolish, not brave."

"I was going to thank you for saving me, but now I think I'll just tell you to go to hell." I turned to leave.

Without warning, he re-appeared in front of me, sporting a gorgeous grin.

I hated that grin. I hated how he could get under my skin so easily. "Get out of my way, or I'm going to rip your throat out. And for the record, no, I'm not afraid of you. I might be young, but I'm not helpless. Try anything, and you'll regret it."

The smile on his face withered and died. "I didn't mean to offend you. I'm very much aware you're an Alpha-born, and you handled yourself well that night. However, I've had the sense that you've been looking for me."

"Looking for you?" The sudden change in topic threw me off for a moment. "Why would I do that?"

He tilted his head to the side. "Come with me. I want to show you something."

I clasped my fingers behind my back. "Aren't you the one who just said I was foolish? Why would I go with you?"

"There isn't a full moon tonight," he answered as he stepped past me. "I also said you handled yourself well against that Bleeder. I'm sure you could do the same with me, but it won't come to that. I have no intention of feeding on you, Elinor." He stopped walking and looked over his shoulder. "Come, it'll be sunrise soon." He paused, waiting for me to make up my mind.

Against my better judgment, I decided to go with him. I knew what he was. I knew the darkness that resided in him. But now I understood all too well that vampires didn't own the monopoly on darkness.

I saw it the moment Council Member Levi told me to kill Meeka.

We traveled in companionable silence, and I took the time to really study him. We walked for what felt like an hour at least. While I should have been worried about where he was taking me, I wasn't. I noticed his gaze was never steady, always on the alert for danger.

I felt safe around this man, but it was just one more thing about him that puzzled me.

I had thought he was near flawless until I spotted a scar peeking out from below the neck of his cloak. It was very thin and pale, and I couldn't help wondering how he'd got it.

His gaze turned my way suddenly.

I looked away. "So, um, what's your name? Since you know mine," I asked quickly to avoid any awkwardness.

He smiled at me again.

"After all," I added, "I think it's only fair I know it, since you're dragging me through the forest to Goddess knows where."

"My name is William, but everyone calls me Will." He reached out and grabbed my arm when I tripped and almost fell. Using just his upper body strength, he helped me stand upright again. "Be careful, Elinor. I don't want to see you wounded again."

He kept saying things like that, things that made me wonder if he cared about me.

I couldn't help shivering a little as I thought about the size and strength of his upper body. I looked down at his fingers, still wrapped around my elbow. His hands weren't cold like they'd been the night he 'd saved me, which surprised me.

His touch felt . . . warm.

He released me, and his hand returned to the cover of his cloak.

I mentally shook my head, unable to believe what I had just felt.

All vampires were cold to the touch—they were all dead, after all. Then again, there was a lot about them we didn't know. Vampires were so cloaked in mystery, it was difficult to tell fact from fiction.

At that moment, I realized something else. I'd been so caught up in the excitement of seeing him again that I hadn't realized my heartbeat wasn't the only one I could hear. My eyes widened as I began to worry that I'd placed myself in yet another dangerous position. I stepped away from him. "What are you? You're not a vampire."

He didn't look surprised by my reaction. He looked . . . disappointed. "I assure you, I'm a vampire," he said as he continued to walk. "Just not the kind you're used to."

I fell in stride with him again. "I can hear your heartbeat. I mean, you didn't have a heartbeat before. . . . So how do you have one now? Your hands aren't cold, like those of a corpse. And your eyes are blue. You're nothing like any vampire I've ever seen."

"Please, Elinor, let it go. I'm a vampire, and that's all you need to know. There is a lot that's not known about my kind." He turned to the left. "We're not all the same."

The sound of rushing water met my ears. "Clearly," I mumbled.

He didn't respond.

I had told myself I wanted to see him, to thank him, to learn his name, and be done with the mystery of the blue-eyed vampire. Yet, here I was, more curious than ever. How was this even possible? How could something like this not be widely known? No wonder he didn't smell the same way other vampires did.

I decided to give the topic a rest—for now. I'd hate for him to get angry and for us to end up fighting. That would be a disaster. Because no matter what he said and how I boasted, in a battle between us, I felt pretty sure I wouldn't emerge the victor.

Maybe that's why you shouldn't have followed him.

We finally came to a stop at a cliff that overlooked the sea. I knew this cliff existed, but I'd never been this far in the forest to actually see it. It wasn't part of my pack's territory.

The panoramic view of the black sky and bright stars above the gentle ocean waves took my breath away. I felt the built-up tension slowly releasing, and my shoulders slumped comfortably.

I would be okay. I could relax.

"Elinor?"

I looked his way, my name but a whisper on his lips.

He sat down and held his hand up to me. "Sit."

I sat down beside him, and we watched the sky in silence.

A shooting star flashed across the heavens, and he leaned over. "Make a wish."

"Pardon?" I glanced his way but quickly turned away when I saw how close his face was to mine. A blush crawled up my cheeks. I bent over to rub my eyes, but I only did it so my hair would fall forward to shield my face.

"Are you sleepy, Elinor?"

Goddess! Would you stop saying my name like that?

"No, I'm okay." I took a deep breath. "Why would I make a wish?"

He reached out and moved my hair back from my face. I made a show of studying the soft waves of the ocean to avoid looking his way. I wasn't sure what to do. I didn't know what to say. I didn't understand why my heart skipped a beat as his finger brushed against my ear.

"It's something humans do when they see a shooting star. They make a wish, hoping it will come true." He tilted his head to the side, watching me.

I pinched the bridge of my nose, unable to endure his gaze any longer. "Please stop doing that."

"Do I make you nervous?"

I decided to ignore his question. "Does wishing on a star actually work?" I asked. I refused to let him get to me, but from the way he chuckled,it seemed like he enjoyed messing with me. I refused to let him get to me. Who'd sent this man into my life, and why was I allowing him to stay?

"I don't know," he finally replied. "I don't think so . . . but it's a beautiful thought, isn't it?"

What would my father say if he could see me now? Here I was, sitting by a cliff with one of the creatures our Guards hunted. On the other hand, here I was, sitting with a creature I'd been taught was consumed by darkness and bloodlust as he talked about how beautiful wishing on a star could be.

"Why did you save me?" I blurted out. "I mean, thank you, but why?"

I waited for him to respond.

Abruptly, he stood. He reached down, clearly expecting me to slide my hand into his.

I sighed, then did it. It seemed evident getting this male to answer my questions would take some work.

He pulled me up gently.

I shivered as he led me closer to the cliff's edge.

"It's almost sunrise," he whispered under his breath before looking out at the incredible view again. "Would you like me to walk you back?"

"So you're just going to ignore my question?"

He sighed as he removed his cloak. He wore clothing similar to the Werewolf Guard's uniform, except his garments were all black. "You don't hold back when you speak, Elinor. It's refreshing. But I really must be going."

I frowned. "Heading home before sunrise? That's good. I'd hate to see you burn to a crisp."

Will chuckled. "Your sarcasm is noted." He stepped back suddenly, and his foot caused some of the earth to break away from the edge of the cliff.

I reacted the same way I would have if it had been anyone else in danger. I rushed forward with my hands outstretched, but then stopped myself just before grabbing him. My hands fell to my side with embarrassment.

He gave me that gentle smile again. "I'll see you soon, Little wolf. Until then, stay out of the forest on a full moon. Okay?"

"I make no promises," I replied with a smile.

He lifted his hand as if to touch my face, but before he could, he leaned backward and dropped off the cliff.

I stepped forward and leaned over the cliff carefully, watching as he disappeared into the water below. I stood there for a moment, waiting to see if he'd resurface, but he didn't.

Will seemed a little eccentric and super-secretive, but I knew I'd be counting the days until I saw him again.

Will

It had been risky to go to the festival, but my urges fought my rational self and won.

I'd wanted to see Elinor, and I'd enjoyed watching her relishing in the joys of life with her friends.

I'd revealed myself to her for a second, and while I'd wanted her to follow me and was relieved that she had, I also worried that she lacked a sense for danger. I'd saved her once before, but I was still a vampire she knew nothing about. And yet, she'd followed me willingly as I'd asked.

I'd told her I wouldn't hurt her, but I could've been lying.

Or perhaps she trusts you, Will, and in that case, what's the problem?

I ran my hands backward over my hair, removing the excess water as I made my way through the forest to the coven. Everything about this situation was confusing. A strange heat radiated through my chest when I thought of how it seemed like she felt at ease with me. But what if that wasn't what it was? What if she just overestimated her ability to protect herself against me?

For a second, I'd scared her when she'd noticed my heartbeat, and when she'd thought I wasn't a vampire because of it . . . well, as understandable as her response was, it had stung. My kind said the same about me, that my heartbeat meant I wasn't a true vampire. It was just one more reason they disliked me.

But even after that, Elinor had sat with me. The girl didn't hesitate to speak her mind, that was for sure, and I couldn't help but like her more for it. Being who I was, very few of my own kind were themselves around me, and even fewer felt the need to speak honestly and not say what they thought I wanted to hear.

But she still had no idea who I truly was, how dangerous it was for us to be friends. How would she react if she ever found out?

No doubt she'd reconsider having anything to do with me.

Or would she?

So far, she'd done nothing the way I'd expected her to. She wasn't like anyone I'd ever met before, and the more I discovered about her, the more I wanted to know. From whispers, I knew she had a reputation for defiance, or at least defiance in the eyes of some, but to me it looked like she just lived authentically.

To me, her ability to unapologetically stand up for herself was a trait for an older soul, someone who'd lived and experienced how cruel this world was and recognized the need for strength and honesty in word and deed.

How much would she grow when faced with reality outside of this small town? How far could our friendship go?

Maybe I was being selfish, knowing the risks of our friendship more than she and choosing to not stay away. But keeping my distance was no longer an option. I was fine being selfish if it meant learning more about her. For the first time, this dull world held a little light for me. I couldn't let that go. It was a risk, but what was life without risk?

And a risk like Elinor . . . that was a risk worth taking.

That little wolf had sunk invisible hooks into me, and I had no desire to break free of them. Still, that rebellious streak of hers could become a problem. If the night she was attacked by Bleeders was any indication, she had more than a fair chance of getting herself in to trouble that might leave more than just a few scratches. I'd have to keep an eye on her, just in case.

Her light was far too bright to be put out.

Elinor

I slowly strolled back through the woods until I made it back to the festival. By the time I returned, the darkness was slowly fading as it made way for the dawn.

Many people had already left, leaving mainly those who were intoxicated and the die-hard partiers behind to carry on. It didn't take long for me to spot Skye and Theanos, considering Theanos's wings were still proudly on display.

"Hey, where have you been?" Skye asked as she leaned against Theanos, her eyes glazed and her words slurred. I eyed a stain on her dress from where she must've spilled her drink. But it was her bruised knuckles that had me wondering what I'd missed.

"She got into it with a kitsune," Theanos explained as he threw his arm over her shoulder to help keep her standing upright.

I shook my head but smiled.

Skye giggled. "I-I won fair and square." Then she leaned towards me and narrowed her eyes. "You didn't answer my question."

I had no idea what she had won, but she looked happy about it. "I was just wandering around," I replied, looking around the now trash-covered town. "Where is Cyrus?" The moment I turned around to look, I had to step back.

Theanos stood directly in front of me, his face inches away from mine, his nostrils flaring.

"What the hell are you doing, sniffing me like that?" I snapped.

He stepped back, his mouth gaping open.

I quickly realized I still had a faint smell of Will on me. I hadn't even noticed it, and as drunk as Skye was, she probably hadn't either.

He arched a brow at me. "Well, well, well, Ms. Blackwood. You're not at all who—"

I punched him in the gut and while I didn't do it hard enough to hurt him, it did knock the wind out of him.

Theanos hunched forward with a groan.

Cyrus swooped in from above and landed gracefully, his wings flapping before disappearing into his back. "What the hell is going on?" he grumbled as he joined us. "What did you do?" he asked Theanos.

He grimaced. "You saw her punch *me*, right? So why am I the one being accused of something?" He glanced my way quickly. "I like you, Elinor. You're not at all what I expected." He waved a finger at me. "You have a curious spirit, and I like that." His knowing smirk grew wider.

"What about me, then?" Skye pulled away and stared up at him. "I'm only the one who's been drinking with you all night. And why is it that you're not drunk?"

Theanos tapped her nose with a finger. "Oh, my darling Skye . . . you, I plan on marrying someday. Our children will be simply stunning, with my good looks and your beautiful skin and eyes." He took her hand and kissed the back of it.

I could have sworn I heard Cyrus growl.

Theanos winked at him playfully before releasing Skye's hand. "I see why you prefer it here, brother."

"Yes," Cyrus replied. "There's life here."

Just then, a woman and a siren began to sing together, drawing our attention to them. The differences in the women's voices made for a beautifully captivating melody, and all those who remained at the festival stopped what they were doing to listen. Their song echoed around us, and I found myself wrapping my arms around myself, a feeling of comfort overwhelming me. The darkness of the night was vanishing as dawn drew nigh, and it almost seemed as if the women were the ones calling it forward.

"I should get home," I said softly.

Skye wrapped her arm around my waist. "Me too. I've had enough."

I placed my hand under her arm to help keep her upright.

Cyrus's wings appeared again. "Yeah, that's a good idea." He walked over to us, then stopped suddenly.

My eyes widened for a moment as he inhaled deeply. *Shit, he's going to smell Will on me as well!*

"Oh, come on," Theanos suddenly yelled as he walked over to Cyrus and threw his arm over his shoulder. His blond hair flew into Cyrus's face, and he winked at me. "Why does the party have to end? We should find a bar or something."

Cyrus shook his head. "This isn't the Demon Realm, Theanos. People here need sleep."

"That's rather boring, don't you think?" Theanos countered.

Cyrus just shook his head, and took Skye from me, walking away with her slowly, her head resting against him. "Come on, we're leaving," he called behind him.

I walked silently by Theanos's side while Cyrus and Skye walked ahead of us, but my mind was on Will. It was as if I was still feeling his warm hand on me.

A vampire with a beating heart . . .

"Fine, we can continue the party at Skye's house," Theanos suggested.

Cyrus shook his head again. "Over my dead body. You're not sleeping anywhere near Skye." He cleared his throat and added, "Or Elinor."

"Uh-huh," I shot back. "Thanks for looking out for me. I appreciate it."

"Is he always like this?" Theanos whispered to me.

I nodded.

"No, I'm not. You bring out the worst in me," Cyrus accused.

I chuckled at their brotherly banter.

Despite the way Cyrus acted, I knew he was happy his brother was here. It felt good to know he had someone from his blood family he could call on if needed. The distance between Cyrus and Skye, and Theanos and me grew the further we walked. When we were far enough away from Cyrus and Skye, I quickly tapped Theanos's shoulder. "Don't say anything to Cyrus, please."

He smirked. "I don't intend to. You're a grown woman. You can do whatever you wish, with whomever you wish." His smile grew further. "From whichever species you wish."

"It's not like that," I replied.

He rolled his eyes. "If it wasn't, you wouldn't be blushing right now."

I bit down on my lip. "It's a long story." I waited until Cyrus moved a little further away from us before speaking again. "He saved me from being killed by a Bleeder."

"What? Really?" Theanos placed his hand on my arm, and we stopped talking. "A Skin saved you by killing one of his own?"

"Yeah, if it hadn't happened to me, I wouldn't have believed it either."

His eyes darted to the side thoughtfully as we continued walking. "Strange."

Oh, you have no idea.

"Does Skye know?"

"Know what?" I asked.

"Does she know that Cyrus is in love with her?"

"Oh . . ." I nodded. "I think it's pretty obvious to everyone else, but no, I don't think she knows. And I don't think he knows that she loves him as well. They're both quite blind about it. But is that even possible for Cyrus and you? Is love something you guys are capable of? You know, being sex demons and all."

Theanos nodded vigorously. "Of course, it is. Demons do feel emotions—some of them at least. While it's still not the same as with humans or supernaturals, we are capable of love. For many demons, loyalty is to them what love is to you guys. They feel a deep sense of loyalty to their clan, their family, and their king."

For the first time since I met him, I sensed a seriousness

about Theanos. I frowned. Right now, he looked every inch the powerful demon he was.

"My mother must never find out about this." He looked my way.

My heart constricted at the weight of his piercing stare.

Theanos sighed heavily. "She can't know that Skye is the reason Cyrus doesn't want to return home to become her successor. If she finds out, I have no doubt my mother *will* try to kill both Skye and you."

We walked in silence for a moment, his words driving worrisome thoughts into my mind. The idea of Cyrus leaving one day—willingly or not—troubled me. Especially now that I knew he was in the same situation I was in, having someone else's plan for his life forced onto him.

Theanos sighed. "I'm also worried about what will happen to Cyrus if Skye should ever find her mate. He's a powerful demon—the son of the Demon King and a Sin—but you two are what's keeping him grounded."

I didn't know what to say as my anxiety worsened. I'd always known of Cyrus's strength. While I hadn't seen how powerful he was firsthand, it wasn't hard to figure out. Especially now that I knew he was the son of the Demon King.

I suddenly felt exhausted. Between the mystery that was Will and now this, I felt as if I'd prefer to sleep for eternity instead of facing the possible negative outcome of all of this.

Still, even knowing how badly my father would react if he found out about my friendship with a vampire, I couldn't make myself avoid Will.

I didn't want to avoid him—I wanted to know exactly what he was.

17

ELINOR

I found myself back on that cliff face again, with Will. He was about to leave, but this time, he held out his hand, silently asking me to go with him. I reached for him, but a barrier rose up between us, stopping me. I stretched and almost reached him. . . . My dream began to slip away, and no matter how I tried to hold onto it, I eventually woke up.

The sound of birds chirping was the first thing I heard. When I opened my eyes, I had to quickly close them as sunlight burned my irises. I groaned and turned my back to the window.

When I opened my eyes again, I came face-to-face with Skye's accusing brown eyes. "Um, morning," I mumbled and sat up.

She didn't respond. Instead, she proceeded to fluff her pillow until-without warning-she hit me over the head with it.

"Hey, what the hell is wrong with you?!" I asked.

Her eyes narrowed even further, and she smacked me again.

This time I was ready for her. I blocked the pillow from hitting me in the face and grabbed it away from her.

"Did you really think I wouldn't notice?" she yelled as she tried to take the pillow back.

"Skye, have you completely lost your mind? What are you talking about?"

She stopped fighting and fell still, her chest rising and falling rapidly, then her hand shot out and punched me in the side.

I yelped.

"What am I talking about?" she fumed. "What am I talking about?! I'm talking about the vampire that I can smell on you!"

My heart stopped beating as her voice echoed through the room. I quickly covered her face with the pillow and pushed her down onto the bed. I took a quick whiff of myself as I recalled falling asleep the moment we had gotten home from the festival.

I still smell like him.

"Be quiet, Skye," I demanded through clenched teeth before removing the pillow from her face.

She took a deep breath dramatically. "Cyrus and Theanos aren't here, and neither is Mother." She sat up. "So, would you like to explain to me why you smell like a vampire?" Her nose scrunched up. "There's something off about the scent, too. You weren't fighting a Bleeder, that's for sure, so you owe me an explanation. Where did you go last night when you left the festival?"

I sat there for a moment as I gathered my thoughts, my

mind still a little foggy. Finally, I started from the beginning, explaining to Skye what had happened that night, with my father, with the Bleeder . . . with Will.

I hadn't told anyone the details about what had happened that night. Everyone knew the reason I'd run off was because my father had tricked me into believing I stood a chance at becoming a Guard.

I filled in the rest of the story for her—how I'd been attacked by the Bleeder and then when another one arrived, it had been killed by Will. I told her about the way he'd stayed with me until I healed enough to make it home and how he had followed me until I was back in my territory.

She listened quietly as I continued the story, moving on to last night and the chat I had with him in the forest. I told her about his soulful blue eyes, but I kept the information about his warm touch and his heartbeat to myself. Until I understood exactly what it all meant, there was no sense in causing Skye unwarranted concern. She would only worry that he might not be a vampire at all.

The same thought had been on my mind since I had felt his touch. Despite the fangs and red eyes I'd seen behind the blue, I had a hard time thinking of him as a vampire. And I also knew I was getting a little too attached to him. My curiosity had grown into something else—interest, attraction —but I couldn't let it go anywhere.

Unfortunately, I just couldn't stop thinking about him, no matter how hard I tried.

After I finished talking, Skye just looked at me. Finally, she laid back on her bed and sighed loudly. "I didn't think I'd ever say this, but . . . you like him. You *finally* like someone, and he's not even a werewolf."

I laid on my stomach beside her and closed my eyes. "I don't like him, Skye. Not in the way, you're referring to. I'm just curious about him. He saved me when he could have killed me and just . . . I don't know, there's something about him."

She didn't reply.

I opened my eyes to find her studying me. "What?"

She continued to stare for a moment until the corner of her lips arched with a smile. "You don't even believe what you just said. You just don't want to admit out loud that there is a part of you that likes him. And that's okay." She turned to stare up at the ceiling. "I get it. Saying it out loud makes it all real, and then there is no going back. Especially when you know you can never be together."

I could tell she was referring to herself and Cyrus, and I recalled finding them together in the forest after Cyrus had returned from the Demon Realm. I hadn't missed the tension between them. Maybe they weren't as blind to each other's attraction as I'd thought.

"It's too early for me to be speaking about feelings." I rubbed at my eyes as the memory of Will jumping off the cliff resurfaced. "I know little to nothing about him, but . . . I enjoy his company. No matter how brief our meetings have been. To him, I'm not just a female firstborn—I'm a girl, a wolf. I don't feel my firstborn status, and all the pressure it brings with it, bearing down on me when I'm around him."

"I think I understand," Skye murmured.

My conversation with Theanos about Skye and Cyrus replayed in my mind, and I turned onto my side to look at her. "Have you ever thought about finding your mate?"

"A little bit. He's not from this pack, or I would have met

him already, and I don't plan on venturing to other packs any time soon in search of him. I wanted to at one point. In fact, I used to look forward to the day I'd meet him." She turned onto her side as well, a few curls falling over her face. "However, now I know I can love and be loved without finding the one made for me."

I nodded in response. "I feel the same. My father acts like I'll never find happiness or live a good life unless I find my mate." I growled. "I've been able to breathe for a little while since he's been away, but when he returns, I know he'll be dragging me to meet another pack."

"I don't care if it happens to me or not," Skye said. "My mother had me outside of a mate bond. She never met her mate, and she's doing just fine." She paused. "Can you imagine if both of us found our mates and had to separate?"

I frowned. "Let's not even talk about it."

She laughed. "Okay then, can you imagine your mother finding out about Will? Let's talk about that for a minute. That would be the last straw - she'd finally lose it."

I shook my hand dismissively as I laughed along with her. While it might indeed push my mother to the brink of insanity, my father would be the bigger problem. "She's not the issue. It's my father—he'd kill us both." My face fell as I thought about it. How would he react if he found out about Will? Would he truly kill me? I would have disgraced the precious Blackwood name.

"Hey . . ." Skye placed her hand on my cheek. "For now, just do what makes you happy. It seems like everyone else does, sometimes at your expense. This town is so boring anyway. You and your vampire lover should spice things up." She giggled.

I covered her mouth quickly, as the sound of someone walking outside the house registered in my mind. I hurried out of bed and rushed to the front door, worried that someone had overheard Skye's words.

I threw the door open and found myself face-to-face with Connor's chest.

"Good, you're awake," he said. He looked over my shoulder as Skye appeared. "We need you back at the house, Elinor. Something has happened."

"What?" I asked as Skye walked back into the house to grab our cloaks. "Did my father return?"

Connor shook his head, the muscles in his jaw clenching with anger. "No, he hasn't. But someone was murdered last night. One of our own was killed at the festival."

Elinor

My fists clenched and unclenched as Connor covered the dead body once more. While I hadn't personally been close to the young male victim or his family, he certainly hadn't deserved to die like this.

"He was just a child," I said through gritted teeth, turning my back to the body on the table.

"His mother and father were told to wait at home." Nurse Hilary pressed her fingers into the corner of her eye, and I noted how exhausted she seemed. "I told them we'd have a report for them soon, but I'm not sure how I'll be able to break this news to them."

Skye and my mother stood by the door, both their eyes

full of tears. They had known the young boy well. I knew the gruesome sight of his mutilated corpse would be imprinted into my memory forever, and I'm sure they both felt the same.

"A vampire did this, right?" my mother asked softly.

Nurse Hilary shook her head. "I don't think so," she answered, "His body was completely drained of blood, but there are no bite marks."

I felt a sudden headache coming on.

"How is that even possible?" Skye looked from Nurse Hilary to Connor and then back again. "What creature can drain someone of their blood without leaving a wound? It makes no sense."

"Still, maybe it *could* have been a vampire. There's so much we don't know about them," I said. I immediately froze, realizing I had spoken my thoughts out loud.

"What makes you say that?" Connor asked, folding his arms over his chest.

I kept thinking of something Will had said, that there were many things we didn't know about vampires. If they successfully concealed beating hearts and warm hands, who knew what they were really capable of? Not many other creatures were known to drain their victim's blood completely. "There's just still a lot of mystery about what vampires can and can't do. What other creature could have done this, Connor?"

He sighed as he pinched his chin, his eyes darting down to the ground. "I'm not sure. A witch, perhaps, or maybe a black magic user."

"That's true," Nurse Hilary added. "There were so many creatures at the festival last night. We can't go making accusations without being sure." She removed the apron she wore. "I'll go speak to the family. But with Alpha Grayson away, who will conduct the burial? It's best to have it done as soon as possible."

"I'll do it," I answered, after a moment of silence. "Jackson is still too young. Is that okay?"

My mother nodded.

I tried not to grip my dress with panic. I'd seen my father conduct countless burials, and there wasn't much to it. Burials were performed at night by the light of the moon. After words of love were spoken over the deceased, my father would shift and initiate a howl. Everyone in the pack would join in the howl in order to send the spirit of our beloved pack member off to the Goddess.

My father wasn't here, but I would do this in his stead.

I looked back at the covered body and clenched my fists. If I were a Guard, I'd stop at nothing to find out who was responsible for this. Because I had a horrible feeling this wouldn't be the last victim.

Elinor

After the last werewolf left, I turned away from the grave and decided to take a walk in the forest.

My body felt numb at how emotional it had all been. My eyes were still stinging with tears I'd had to hold back as I assumed the role of Alpha for those few hours. I had to be everyone's strength as they fell apart, and it had been painful. But I felt relieved that this part was over. Now, we had to find out who had done this. There hadn't been a death in our pack for almost two years, and the last one had been from natural causes. My father would be livid when he got back, but I didn't want to think about it right now. I just wanted to feel.

I wished I could shift and go for a run, feeling the earth beneath my feet as I raced against the wind, but I'd hate to ruin the dress my mother had given me.

Seeing all those wolves mourning had reminded me of Meeka. I swallowed hard, trying desperately to hold back a sob as I reached out and braced myself on the trunk of a tree. I hadn't been able to bring myself to attend her burial. Because of me, she'd died. Because of my weakness, she died at the hand of Levi.

I stood up straight after a moment, as my chest felt unexpectedly tight. I took in a few sharp breaths before moving forward. I stopped in my tracks as a painful howl pierced the silent night, and I knew I was hearing a mother's lament. The boy's name had been Keith, and he had been a promising fighter. In his mother's cry, we all realized what we had lost.

So many bright flames die out early . . .

There was so much beauty in this world, but also so much darkness, anger, and hatred. I was not naïve. I knew there couldn't be one without the other. There had to be a balance. But sometimes, it was just so hard to accept.

I lifted my dress as I continued on my slow stroll—until I came to the end of pack territory. I stood there, just over the line, then fell to my knees and let the tears I had been holding back finally fall like drops of rain onto the ground. Sometimes witnessing such injustice drained a person's energy and made them feel helpless.

I hated that feeling. I hated feeling helpless.

I covered my mouth as I screamed, and I continued to do so as my body shook. I didn't care if anyone saw me. But that was before I heard his voice.

"Little Wolf?"

I got up quickly and began wiping at my tears.

Will stepped forward.

"What are you doing here?" I asked, turning my back to him so I could try and get a hold of myself before he saw.

I realized it then—with the way my tense shoulders relaxed—I had come into the forest hoping he'd show up. But now that he was here, I was torn between wanting him to stay and hating that he had caught me crying. I inhaled deeply and turned to face him.

His hair was combed neatly back, and this time he wore the same black, skin tight breeches and shirt without the cloak. "Why are you crying?"

"You're in werewolf territory. If someone sees you here, they will have all the right to kill you. Why are you here?" My words came out a lot sharper than I'd intended.

His brows pulled together for a second. He pointed to the deep claw marks on the tree trunk to my left, a sign that marked the beginning and end of our territory. "I'm standing outside your territory, not in it. But I have to ask again . . . why are you crying, Elinor? Did someone hurt you?"

My jaws clenched as my hand by my side twitched. Concern showed in his eyes, but was it real? I looked away. I couldn't let this happen. I couldn't grow close to him, not when one of his kind had just killed one of mine.

You don't know if that's true, Elinor.

I took a deep breath and let it out. No, I didn't know if a

vampire had killed Keith. I growled, angry at myself for thinking about using Keith's death to justify why I wanted to end what had started here.

Will finally spoke, "I came to tell you to stop coming so deep into the forest."

I froze, my brows knitting as I looked up. "Excuse me?"

He clasped his hands behind him as he glanced at the claw marks on the tree trunk. "You need to trust me. It's not safe for you to be out here."

"Who do you think you are?"

His expression didn't change when faced with my anger.

"This is my *home*," I went on. "I live in the woods. I'm a firstborn and fully capable of taking care of myself. Who are you to tell me where I should and shouldn't go, or what's dangerous for me?"

"Elinor, I know you're upset about something. But I need you to see reason and trust me."

I laughed, but it held no humor. What had possessed him to come to me tonight, trying to control me? It was bad enough when I got this kind of attitude from my father. But coming from Will—well, it hurt. "Trust you? I don't even know you. I don't know what you are, and you refuse to tell me." I crossed my arms over my chest. "Did you come all this way to see me, just so you could tell me what to do? Huh? I'm not weak, Will. I have never been."

He frowned.

The silence of the night stretched on, neither of us saying anything.

I wanted this conversation to be over because I sensed an argument on the horizon. The pent-up emotions I'd been holding in were close to boiling over. And after conducting a burial for a young pup who should have had his whole life before him, all I wanted to do was punch something.

I was angry with Will because I now understood that I'd never be more than just a fragile little wolf to him.

I didn't need his protection or anyone else's.

I bit down on my lip as I tried to control the rage that grew with every breath I took. "These woods are just as dangerous for you, Will, being this close to wolf territory."

He inhaled deeply. "I'm here to feed. That is why I'm here. And that is how I know Bleeders are on their way here now. That is why I want you to go! Stop being stubborn, wolf, and go home!" Those blue eyes I had become so accustomed to seeing rapidly turned red.

My expression fell as he stepped toward me. I understood at that moment that once again, he was only trying to protect me. My anger dissipated a little, but not completely. Trying to scare me was the worst thing he could have done. I tilted my head back to stare up at him, while my nails elongated by my side and my eyes changed to black.

His body was almost touching mine, and this time, I felt no warmth radiating from him. He was cold. The memory of Keith's cold body flashed in my mind, and I was unable to stop the expression of disgust from appearing on my face.

It didn't go unnoticed by him.

Unfortunately, I was sure he'd misinterpreted it as disgust towards him, and when he stepped back, my suspicion was confirmed. I felt the connection that had been forming between us fall and shatter as his lips parted, and I glimpsed his fangs. "If you're trying to scare me, Will, you're doing a terrible job at it. I'm not the weakling you think I am."

He tilted his head to the side.

I ground my feet into the earth beneath me as black veins appeared on his neck leading up to his cheeks. His jaw snapped, and I couldn't help the jolt that went through my body.

Is he really going to attack me?

His mouth began to stretch open, his fangs on full display as his tongue swiped over his lips. "You should be afraid, Little Wolf. I've never called you weak, but don't think for a second that you can win against me." He leaned down until his cheek was beside mine. "My own kind fears me, and you should, too."

I felt his tongue flick against my ear. I clenched my fist and punched him in the chest with as much power as I could muster. He was thrown back a few steps, but that was all. I held my shock inwards because it seemed like I had barely touched him.

"I came here out of concern for you," he said. "You don't know what's happening outside of this town or the danger you're risking. Stay out of the woods, and stay away from me!"

"Gladly!" I yelled back, my voice echoing around us. "I was a fool to think that you—" I stopped myself from finishing the statement.

His eyes widened as the black veins on his skin started to fade.

I inhaled deeply, letting go of the anger. "Don't you worry about me, Will. I'll stay away from you. But don't hunt anywhere near this territory again if you want to remain living." Then I turned and strode away.

I kept moving until I could no longer feel his eyes on me. I didn't understand why my chest ached so much. All I wanted at this moment was to crawl into bed and sleep for an eternity.

Why had we just argued like that?

I reached up and covered my face at the memory, at the things I had said to him. I hadn't been angry at him—I was just angry at everything. But I'd lost it when he said I should stay out of the woods. I lived here, damn it, and while I knew what he meant, the thought of not being able to run in my own pack's territory just rubbed me the wrong way.

Maybe this was for the best. Our friendship had been doomed from the start. So why did it feel like I had just lost someone dear to me?

Will

$\mathcal{I}$ picked up a chair and threw it across the room, the wood shattering on impact. "Get out!"

The vampire serving as my maid flinched, frozen in shock. I tilted my head to the side and deliberately allowed my eyes to shift to blue even while my veins turned to black.

"I said get out!"

She'd already been backing away in fear at the sight of my blue eyes and was gone within seconds.

With my fists clenched, I closed my eyes and tried to ground myself. I couldn't recall the last time I was unable to contain my anger. Elinor was as infuriating as she was beautiful, but I'd pushed her.

But I'd only made matters worse.

I was a fool to think that you—

That was what she'd said, but what else was she going to say? What had she thought? Was she going to say she thought this friendship between us could work? Had I just lost her for good?

The way she'd flinched at my closeness . . . it had stung, more than I thought it could.

Laying my palm on my chest, I felt the stillness inside me, my flesh cold. Had she been repulsed by me this entire time and I hadn't realized, too caught up in my fascination of her to see that it was one sided?

No, that wasn't it. If Elinor hadn't shared my feelings at least to some extent, she wouldn't have entertained our friendship. No, something tonight had upset her, something big enough to make her question whether I was really someone she could talk to.

Just the thought that something or someone had upset her or her hurt was enough to give me the intense urge to strangle whoever it was who had caused her pain.

Seeing her tears had shaken me to my core even though my heart had been still. Elinor was the first bright light I'd seen in a long time, and unlike other dark creatures who would run or seek to put it out, it kept pulling me in.

I'd long since grown tired of the darkness of vampirism. Now, I wanted peace and light, and she offered that. If what she wanted was freedom, I could give that to her.

I just need to find out what happened to cause this argument, and then I'd fix it.

18

___

SKYE

I sat down and pulled my hair into a bun, sighing loudly. I smiled at the spotless living room before getting up to take a bath.

I hadn't been able to stop thinking about the vampire Elinor had told me about two days ago. It was clear she liked him.

But I worried about her. This was a vampire we were talking about, after all. Who knew what his real intentions were? Yes, I was aware I was judging the guy before I knew him. And I knew I could be wrong. After all, Cyrus was a demon, and look how amazing he turned out to be. I trusted Elinor to know what she was doing, but was it wise for her to be friends with someone like him? And what was up with him having blue eyes?

First, she had been attacked by Bleeders, who were hunting very close to our territory. Thankfully, Will had been there to save her—he had my respect for that. But was that just lucky timing . . . or had he planned the whole thing just to gain her trust?

I rested my head back against the edge of the steel tub and listened as the water splashed around with my movements. I closed my eyes for a moment and sighed. Well, she actually met him long before then, on the road heading home that one day. But why was he hanging around our town so much in the first place?

Now a young child's life had been taken by something that had drained him of blood. It all seemed a little too fishy for me.

I jumped as I heard the front door open and close. I quickly grabbed my towel and wrapped it around me before heading out of the bathroom.

"C-Cyrus?" I stuttered as I entered the living room and found him standing by the door.

He seemed to be sweating profusely, his hair damp and his white cotton shirt sticking to his body.

I tried to avoid looking at the toned muscles of his chest showcased by the wet shirt and instead focused on his droopy eyes. "Cyrus, what's going on?" I stepped forward.

He quickly raised his hand to stop me. "I'm fine. I just feel a little under the weather. I just need a moment." He inhaled deeply, and his nose crinkled as he grimaced. "May I have some water?"

I quickly filled a glass while keeping an eye on him.

He leaned against the door, his chest rising and falling rapidly as he closed his eyes.

I'd seen him like this twice before, and just like those times, my heart hammered away with panic.

Why do you keep doing this?!

I walked back over to him and put the glass in his hand. "I know what's happening, Cyrus. You can't keep doing this."

He pulled his lips away from the glass. His eyes were changing from gray to black and somehow, he looked even paler than he'd appeared just moments ago. "I'm fine," he replied weakly.

My heart sank. I had to fight the urge to smack him the way I usually did. "You're not fine!" I growled through clenched teeth. "You need to stop starving yourself, Cyrus. How long have you gone without feeding this time for it to get this bad? Huh?"

He looked away.

I smacked his shoulder. "Answer me! You can't keep doing this!"

He looked back at me and gave me another weak smile as I adjusted my towel.

I wasn't at all bothered by him seeing me in this way. We'd grown up together, and I was sure he'd seen me naked at one point or another after shifting. "You need to take better care of yourself. I swear to the Goddess, I won't tell you again. You can't survive on only human food. Look at you . . ." I poked his chest. "How long?"

He sighed. "Four months."

I stepped back.

Ever since we were teenagers and his cravings started, he'd been rejecting his incubus side by not feeding. As an incubus, he had to feed on the sexual desire of others to survive. But given the relationship he had with his mother and the fact that he silently detested being an incubus, he went as long as possible between feedings.

I walked away to set the glass down before facing him once more, my arms crossed over my chest. "Why? Why do you insist on doing this? Feeding once every week or two won't kill you, Cyrus. You are what you are, and you need to do what you have to in order to survive."

"I'm fine, Skye. All I need is a minute to rest a little." He turned as if to head to his bedroom.

I quickly ran forward to block his path. I refused to sit by and watch this happen. He was starving himself, hurting himself, and I wouldn't stand for it. "Blow this off as if it's nothing, and I swear I'll go get Elinor. Try telling her you're fine."

He frowned at this, knowing that dealing with Elinor was a completely different story. Whenever Elinor became concerned about someone, she was almost unbearable to be around. Her stubbornness would not permit her to let it go.

"So, what will it be, huh? Should I call for her?"

He leaned forward and placed his hand on my shoulder. "I just need to sleep for a bit, Skye, and I'll be fine. Why can't you trust me on this?"

"Feed on me." The words left my lips before I'd even really thought about it. But even as his eyes lowered and became even blacker, I didn't regret the offer.

His hand fell off my shoulder as he stood up straight. "Don't say that to me . . . ever."

"I mean it. You refuse to feed on a random person, so feed on me." My shoulders slumped somewhat. "Please, I can take it. Let me help you."

Cyrus stepped back, a strained look on his face. "You can't." He turned to leave.

I grabbed his arm to stop him. He pulled away from me, and suddenly, he had me pinned to the wall. I reacted simply on reflex and tried to trip him, but his wings shot out from his back as he grabbed me and flipped us over, so I landed on the floor beneath him.

Something fell to the ground and shattered in the room—no doubt his wings had knocked something over—but I was too transfixed by the emotions in his eyes to think about anything else.

"You have no idea what you're asking me, Skye." His eyes drifted from my face to my lips and then down to my hand gripping my towel.

I reached up to touch him.

Without warning, he grabbed my left hand as it moved toward his face, pulled my other hand away from the towel, and pinned them both above my head. He closed his eyes for a moment, his nostrils flaring as he inhaled deeply. "I can't feed on you, Skye." His eyes opened. "I won't be able to stop myself."

I swallowed hard as his grip on my hands tightened a little. Of course, he wasn't hurting me. It was the passion and need on his face that was rendering me speechless.

We remained like that for a while, neither of us moving. His breathing was steadily becoming more labored. As his lips parted and I caught a glimpse of his fangs, my eyes widened. My mind and body were at war—my mind telling me this was a mistake, my body saying something else altogether.

I didn't know if he was the one doing it, but a burning need began in my heart and began coursing through the rest of my body. He inhaled deeply once more, and my stomach clenched as a growl slipped from his lips.

All I wanted to do was help him. He had no idea how

much it hurt me to see him like this. How much it hurt to know that he hated a part of himself.

He looked away from me, his face turning red as he fought against what he needed—what he wanted.

I'd never been able to admit, even to myself, that I'd always had feelings for him. There was a time when I thought he saw me as nothing more than a sister, but over the years, I could tell, sometimes from the way he'd look at me or from certain things he'd say, that there might be more than familial love and friendship between us.

Although he was basically a part of our pack, I knew Alpha Grayson would never allow there to be anything between us. So, I kept my thoughts and feelings to myself.

But I couldn't anymore. "Cyrus, I need to tell you—"

"Shhh," he whispered as he released one of my hands. He cupped my cheek, and my body heated from the inside out as he pressed his thumb to my lips.

I clenched my fists, not knowing what to do as he slowly lowered himself until his body was pressed to mine. He released my other hand, and I whimpered as his warm fingers slid down my body to my thigh. I could feel the heat his body produced through my towel, and it was as if I was surrounded by warmth. I was entirely at his mercy like this, trapped on the floor with nothing between us but my towel and his wet shirt.

I'd never been touched like this. I'd never wanted—no, needed—anyone the way I needed him right now. His wings flapped above us, and I pressed my legs to the side of his body.

"I don't want to hurt you," he told me, his breath fanning my lips since he was now only inches away from my face.

"You won't, I promise."

A pulse-like shockwave left his body and seeped into me. I hastily grabbed his shoulders as desire blossomed in my core. I arched off the ground, my body shaking violently, and my legs at his sides squeezed against him even harder.

My thoughts became foggy. He caressed my cheek with his hand, but it felt as if he was touching every inch of my body. My eyes opened slowly as I felt my towel finally come undone. His mouth was open, his eyes now wide with color returning to his cheeks, as he looked me up and down.

I didn't feel ashamed or shy. The way he gazed at me made me feel beautiful—desirable even. I felt a pull on my body, like someone was yanking on a cord attached to me. A moan escaped my lips as I felt him place a gentle kiss on my shoulder.

Then he captured my lips, and my body exploded with raw, untamed lust. I smiled as his tongue darted out to gently flick against my lips, and I opened myself to him.

There was no going back now.

Elinor

A knock came at my door, and I rolled onto my back before sitting up. I sighed and rubbed at my eyes. "Come in."

The door opened, and Jackson poked his little head in. "Sleeping?"

I waved at him to come in. "I'm not. What's wrong? Are you looking for Mother?"

He shook his head, and his curls bounced as he crossed the room to stand before me. His hands were behind his back as he swayed from side to side.

I chuckled. "What's wrong?" He glanced at me from under his lashes, looking so adorable, I couldn't help laughing. "Come on, spit it out now."

"Why—why do you dislike me, Elinor?"

My face fell as I stared at him in shock. "I'm sorry, what? Why would you ever think that?"

He glanced to the side. "Well, you don't . . . play with me, and you don't talk to me." He looked at me once more.

It felt like a hand was squeezing my heart as I saw the tears in his eyes.

Jackson and I had never been close, but a lot of that was due the difference in age between us. While my mother kept him close to her, I was always off with Skye or Cyrus, or doing something that would keep me out of the house entirely. I hated being trapped inside, except when I needed space from everyone. I didn't dislike my brother—I never could—but a bond had just never grown between us.

I reached out and pulled him closer, and he climbed onto the bed with me. "Never think that, do you hear me? I'm your big sister. Of course I love you. I just—" I sighed. "I just get busy doing my own thing sometimes."

"My friends talk to their siblings . . . but we don't talk." He scratched his head sheepishly.

I wondered what had possessed him to come to me about this now. I was happy he had because I'd hate for him to grow up thinking I hated him, but what had brought this on?

He spoke again, "I know I stole the right to be the next

Alpha from you, but I didn't mean to. You can be the Alpha if I give it to you, right?" He half-smiled. "Then, we can talk."

I couldn't look away from the hurt in his eyes, and at that point, my self-loathing knew no bounds. I had no excuse for not bonding with my little brother. How long had he believed I didn't like him? I reached out and pulled him into a hug. "You're my little brother, Jackson. Never doubt that I love you and never, ever offer the position of Alpha to anyone. It's yours, and yours only." I pulled back and wiped a tear from his eye.

Although he looked so much like my father, I knew he had a soft heart like our mother. It was sad to know becoming the Alpha would kill that part of him.

"Can you help me with my studies tomorrow?" he asked shyly.

I nodded and ruffled his hair. "Of course. And how about we go into town afterward and get you some treats? Our secret?"

He nodded vigorously, the sadness in his eyes gone.

I wished I had his ability to forget the things that hurt me so quickly. It had been four days since my argument with Will, and I couldn't help feeling I'd made our argument worse than it had to be.

It hadn't been until the day after our last encounter that I'd realized how much effort he had put into pushing me away. He'd vamped out in an attempt to scare me off. While it had worked to some extent, it had also shown me that maybe I had gotten under his skin, the same way he'd gotten under mine.

"There you are." My mother walked into the room.

Jackson jumped off the bed and ran to her. "Elinor and I are going to get treats tomorrow!"

My mother's brow arched.

I chuckled sheepishly. "That was meant to be a secret, Jackson."

"Sorry." He pouted before looking up at our mother. "Can I still go?"

She nodded, pushing his hair back from his face.

I smiled. She'd done the same thing to me when I'd been his age. Back then, she and I'd been inseparable.

Her expression grew serious as she looked my way. "Your father is back. And he's brought a guest."

My jaws clenched, but I decided to not say anything nasty in response with Jackson watching and listening closely. "I'll be right down."

She turned and left with Jackson.

I slammed my hand down on the bed. She didn't have to tell me who our guest was. A part of me had been expecting it.

Because I knew, without a doubt, that at this moment, there was a firstborn downstairs, waiting to see if I was his mate.

Elinor

After taking a few minutes to prepare myself mentally, I made my way downstairs. At this point, I had to psych myself up even to face my father. As I descended the stairs, I could hear them all speaking in the living room, and I began taking deep breaths. I could smell two unfamiliar wolves as I drew closer to the living room.

Neither of the scents invoked a reaction from me, and I smiled.

Despite Father's best efforts, it looks like my elusive mate will remain a mystery—for now at least.

I entered the living room and found my mother and father seated beside each other.

Two males sat across from my parents, looking like an older and younger version of each other. I only recognized the one male as older because of his salt-and-pepper hair color. The younger male—his son, I assumed—had dark brown locks instead.

They both looked my way the moment I entered the room, their piercing green, calculating eyes boring into me.

"Elinor, let me introduce you to Alpha Kachon and his son, Elijah." My father stood up.

Alpha Kachon and Elijah also stood.

Elijah wasn't as muscular as the typical wolf, but something about his observant gaze had me doubting his smaller stature would ever be a problem. Many people assumed an Alpha had to be big for him to be powerful, but that was not at all true.

He placed his fist over his heart, as did his father, and they both bowed. "It's a pleasure to finally meet you, Elinor."

I responded in the same way, "Likewise, Elijah." I then turned Alpha Kachon. "It's a pleasure to meet you, Alpha Kachon."

"Well, they aren't mated. That's obvious," my mother interjected.

I stood up straight and tried not to smile, even though I

wanted to. I glanced at my father to gauge his reaction to the news.

However, he wasn't looking at me. His eyes were on Alpha Kachon.

I frowned at the nod that passed between them.

"That's of no consequence," Alpha Kachon replied as he sat down. "Alpha Grayson and I have already discussed this possibility."

"I don't understand. Discussed what?" I asked.

Elijah remained standing, looking equally confused.

My father spoke, "Alpha Kachon and I have decided that even if you aren't mated to Elijah, you will still marry him and become the next Luna for the Red Lotus Pack."

My jaws clenched as I tried not to react the way my mind was telling me to. The glare my father sent my way, the one silently telling me to behave *or else*, didn't go unnoticed. I looked over at Elijah.

He stared at his father, his jaws clenched.

It looks like I'm not the only firstborn that has father issues.

"And after Elinor and I are married, what happens if either of us meets our mate? Are we to reject them?" Elijah's voice had dropped.

My respect for him grew. He wasn't about to accept this quietly.

"If we ever get to that bridge, we'll cross it then. Our focus, for now, is for the two of you to be married," Alpha Kachon replied.

I couldn't help myself—I pinned him with a glare I didn't bother to try and hide.

He chuckled, seeming not to care that I was obviously

angry. "Your father told me you're a stubborn girl, Elinor, and very opinionated. I don't mind that. You'll make a wonderful Luna. My people will love you. There is no doubt about that. So maybe this marriage won't be as bad as you think." He leaned forward. "I heard about your exceptional performance in the Guard examinations. I'm sure you understand, however, that once you're married to my son, you'll be required to stand by his side, not go out hunting dark creatures."

I gave him a tight-lipped smile. "Thank you for your kind words, Alpha Kachon." I turned to my father. "May I speak to you in private?"

"We can talk later, Elinor," he replied.

My smile widened. "Are you certain you want me to say what I must right here, Father?"

He exhaled heavily. "Excuse us."

We left the room and made our way upstairs to his office. All the while, I tried my best to avoid foaming at the mouth with rage. How could he do this to me? An arranged marriage! Had he completely lost his mind? Elijah's question about our possible mates was the very reason no one ever arranged marriages between werewolves.

He closed his office door behind him. "Don't start, Elinor."

"How could you?" I asked softly, my voice and tone normal, which I was sure he hadn't been expecting.

He turned to face me, his eyes narrowed. "You're getting older and haven't been able to find your mate. I won't stand for anyone gossiping about my daughter as if she's . . ." He stopped speaking.

I tilted my head to the side. "As if she's what, Father? Broken? Is that it? People are gossiping about me?"

He didn't reply as he walked around his desk to sit down.

I watched him silently, realizing that I didn't know him at all. When I was a girl, before the truth of what being a first-born female entailed was explained to me, I loved my father like no one else.

Back then, I'd been intimidated by him, as most people were, but I loved him. He wasn't just my father, but the Alpha, and I felt proud to be called his daughter. Now all I felt when I thought of him was shame—shame at being related to someone who could do the kind of things he had done to me.

"You know what?" I exhaled. "You and I have never been able to see eye-to-eye on this, and after what you did, we never will." My reference to his trickery during the Werewolf Guard examination had his jaw clenching. "You insist on treating me like a bag of rice you need to sell as soon as possible. And I have no more interest in arguing with you. You're my Alpha, and as I've said before, what you say goes. I will marry Elijah if he wishes to go ahead with the marriage."

He stared at me with confusion as I stepped forward. I knew he was expecting me to argue or throw a fit, but I was done with all of that. And I was done with him. "Just know this. Once I marry Elijah, I will take his name, and I will no longer be your daughter. I have no desire to be associated with someone who could do what you have done to me. "

He didn't respond, and his eyes became unreadable.

I stood there, barely holding on to my composure.

"You did well to conduct Keith's burial," he said abruptly.

I nodded, fine with the change of subject. He appeared to

accept the consequences of his decision, so I'd better get used to it being like this between us until I left.

"Thank you." I meant to walk away at that point, but I couldn't. I needed to know what was going on. "I've had a bad feeling for some time now that you're keeping something a secret, something dangerous. I heard you and Connor talking about it the other night."

He looked away, which merely confirmed my suspicions.

I probed further, "Do you know what killed Keith? Hilary couldn't tell if it was a vampire or not."

"Keith's is the sixth murder so far, and Guards are still looking for the killer."

I felt a little surprised he answered so easily but remained quiet, hoping he'd go into more detail.

He continued, "Out of the six victims, he's the second wolf. The others were two witches, an elf, and a centaur. So far, all we know is that it's not a Bleeder—the bodies would have been more badly damaged. Still, we've noticed a spike in the number of Bleeders in our area, as well."

I frowned. "Maybe it's a Skin?"

He shook his head as he pinched the bridge of his nose.

I noticed the tired look in his eyes. "Was this why you were gone for so long?"

He nodded, then continued, "It's not a Skin. There were no bite marks left on any of the bodies, so it has to be another supernatural. We've been keeping this quiet because if word gets out, it will create a lot of tension among all the supernatural groups in the vicinity. All victims were drained of their blood, yet there were no wounds."

Supernaturals who are friendly with each other could suddenly become suspicious of each other. Fingers will be pointed. Still, people need to be told about this. They need to be on guard.

"I'll be leaving again next week. An Enchanted is being sent from the Council and will be staying a few towns away from here. We're arranging a meeting between all the species who have a victim."

"You're going to increase patrols, though, right? I mean, I know that was already done after I was attacked, but do we have enough men?" I felt a little panicked. Some unknown creature was stalking supernaturals, and even the Guards were at a loss about what exactly they were tracking.

"That'll be taken care of." He sighed. "Darian and his team will be called back to look after the pack while I'm gone."

I wanted to ask why he was being so forthcoming, but I didn't dare, in case he stopped talking. I'd always wanted to be included in what happened in and around the pack.

"Okay," I answered as I turned and started to leave.

My father called out behind me, "Keep this to yourself, Elinor. Cyrus and Skye don't need to know. Not yet."

I nodded, even though I knew it would be nearly impossible to keep something this important from them. "Okay."

Will

After my argument with Elinor, I learned of the wolf who had been murdered during the festival. It all made sense that she'd been so upset and in such a vulnerable place. When I heard that the wolf's body had been drained, her reaction to my proximity made sense. Very few creatures were capable of something like that; I was one of them.

Even though I could understand her revulsion at my species, at what we were capable of, it still stung to be lumped into the same group as the creature who had murdered the wolf—if it turned out a vampire had done it at all.

Without actual bite marks on the body, how could it have been a vampire? Although, if I'd been in Elinor's position—knowing only what she knew of the world and our species—I probably would've reacted the same way.

This town was a delightful example of positive co-existence among supernaturals, but someone was out to disturb that delicate balance. Disruptions to the peace here disturbed my relationship with Elinor, and that alone made me want to track down the culprit and eliminate them myself.

What relationship?

Those words echoed in my mind as I made my way through the forest, and I frowned.

Our friendship, I corrected myself. No matter what we were to each other, the benefit of time and a little more information helped me understand her pain from the night we'd argued.

I'd told her to stay out of the forest, but I knew that was a command she wouldn't obey. The forest was her home, and nothing anyone ever said could keep a woman like Elinor away from her home. At some point, we'd see each other again. Hopefully, when we came face-to-face the next time, she would be willing to forgive me. I refused to let this be our end.

Hopefully, she felt the same.

After some time, I caught onto her scent and smiled. For once, her defiance was working in my favor. Holding my head back, I took a deep breath, separating her scent from all others before following it.

If I let her stay angry at me any longer, I risked losing her for good.

Elinor

I kind of liked the feeling of the damp grass beneath me. It had rained for hours earlier today, but when it had finally stopped, I was able to slip out of the house.

Thanks to the storm, the air felt cool and smelled so fresh. I closed my eyes for a moment as the wind blew across my skin, and when I opened them again, a shooting star shot across the sky.

Will he come?

I bit down on my lip as the sound of crashing waves hit my ears. This was tranquility. This was peace. When I married Elijah—since that was now a done deal—I'd miss this. I'd miss Cyrus, Skye, my other pack members, and my town. I swallowed hard as my emotions started to consume me.

No, I won't cry. Crying will solve nothing. Maybe leaving this town and this pack will be good for me.

After speaking with my father and giving him my nerve-wracking declaration that I would no longer be his daughter, we went back downstairs and discovered that Elijah had also lost the debate with his father.

Then our parents left us alone to *get to know each other*. After ten minutes of awkward silence, we ended up discussing how unfair our situation was. We had that much in common, at least. In fact, I almost felt sorrier for him, especially after I learned he had a girlfriend.

Elijah would be forced to end a relationship with a woman he actually loved to marry me, even though I was not his mate. I shook my head as I listened to the ocean. I couldn't imagine how his girlfriend would feel when she found out and how awkward it'd be when I finally met her. I felt uncomfortable knowing she would have to watch me living out my life with the man she loved.

Sure, she would have had to do the same if he had found his mate, but he hadn't. He'd be marrying someone who wasn't his mate either, someone who was a complete stranger to him.

What'll be worse is the day his mate turns up—if she ever does.

What would happen then, especially if I'd already had a child—or children—by him? My father agreeing to something like this only solidified my belief that he cared about nothing other than seeing me become a Luna for another pack. He saw no other path in life for me, and so he didn't care that this might end badly for me. This was exactly why I needed to see Will tonight. I needed to see him one last time. Our friendship had been doomed from the start, but I didn't want it to end the way I'd left it at our last meeting.

I'd tried for weeks to put meaning to what I felt for him. Actually, I'd avoided admitting what was now suddenly so clear to me. I was intrigued by him, at his way of seeming so normal while also being the strangest person I'd ever known.

Thunder rumbled in the distance, and I sighed. "I know you're there."

A soft chuckle met my ears. I listened to the sound of Will's shoes crunching on the grass as he made his way over to me and sat by my side.

I glanced his way, seeing the black strands of his hair dance wildly in the wind.

"Where have you been?" he asked.

"Where have you been?" I asked back. "You told me to stay away, remember? I was doing what you asked."

He turned to face me. "So, you're doing as you're told now?"

"I'm turning over a new leaf. You're looking at a new Elinor."

"So, why are you here tonight then?" His head slowly tilted to the side as he watched me nervously play with a strand of my hair. I figured this would be a nice spot to relax for a little while." I inhaled. "And you? Why are you here, then? Hunting again?"

"No," he replied simply.

I waited for him to elaborate, but he didn't. "Okay, so why *are* you here?" I sat up finally and brushed the leaves out of my hair. "Don't think for a second you can claim this spot. I really love this place." I smiled at him.

He reached out and removed a leaf I'd missed from my hair, then looked away, turning his attention back to the sky.

I sighed. Getting information out of him was, as always, a task. *Why do I feel like I'm going to miss it?* "Do you always have to be so close-mouthed?"

"Yes. It helps me maintain my mysterious aura." He said it so casually—and with a straight face!

I couldn't help laughing. He smiled, watching me, and I shook my head. "You're impossible," I breathed as a heavy wind blew in from the sea.

However, I was happy he had come. I wasn't sure how to say goodbye to him without telling him about my marriage. Then again, why did I need to keep it a secret? Given the fact that Elijah had a girlfriend, I had a feeling things weren't going to go smoothly. I'm sure everyone would hear about it, wolf or supernatural. Basically, I just wanted to clear the air between Will and me before I started on my journey to become a wife. I frowned then. Somehow, I couldn't picture myself as a wife.

We sat in comfortable silence until it started to rain a little. We remained there, letting the small droplets of water slowly soak us both.

"Do you wish to go home?" Will asked.

"Thanks for asking, instead of telling me to," I answered.

He smiled. "I think I learned the hazards of telling you that at our last meeting." His soft eyes became guarded, and as he looked away, his smile faded.

I wiped the raindrops from my eyes, watching him comb his wet hair back from his face. I couldn't help staring at his stunning side profile. "I'm sorry about the other night. I was upset about—something."

"I know," he replied. "You don't need to apologize." He looked my way.

As I pushed my soaked hair back from my face, I caught the moment his eyes changed from blue to red and then back to blue.

I blinked rapidly, my body growing tense. For the very first time, I realized he probably wanted to feed on me. Why had it never occurred to me before?

I was basically food for him.

I pushed that particular thought away as I prepared to tell him what I'd come here to say. It shouldn't have been this hard, but it was. "I think this will be our last meeting," I forced the words out and waited anxiously for him to reply.

"Have you found your mate, then? You're of age, so I assume you've been looking."

If you mean, am I being forced, then yes.

I shook my head. "No, but . . . this friendship is doomed, Will. You're a vampire, and I'm a werewolf. Nothing good can come from this."

A crease appeared between his brows, but it vanished quickly as it appeared. "I don't agree with you. Our friendship will be a problem for others because they can't see past the stigma placed on vampires. Yes, a lot of my kind are savages, but not all of them are." He tilted his head to the side. "If anyone has an issue with our friendship, I think that's their problem, not ours. Don't you think?"

I smiled. "If only things worked as easily as you make it sound. Do you make it a habit of becoming friends with your food?"

"Yes." He inhaled deeply, and this time when he frowned, the crease between his brows remained. "I do actually, but not with my food, but with people worth my attention." He reached out and pinched my chin.

At that moment, my heart threatened to stop beating.

"Maybe in another time, we'd . . ." His words trailed off.

My heart skipped a beat as his hand fell away from my chin. What had he been about to say?

The silence stretched out between us before he looked away.

"I wish I could tell what you're thinking sometimes," I muttered.

He smiled and shook his head, sending raindrops flying from his hair. "Trust me, Elinor. You would not like to know what's going on inside my head."

"I think I would." I reached out and poked his chest. "Do you think your thoughts would scare me?"

He glanced down at his chest before looking up at me with a wicked grin. "I'm certain of it. There are many things in this world that are capable of making you shiver and shake. And many of those things I've done."

My brow arched with curiosity. "Tell me one thought you think might scare me." I leaned forward and whispered, "Try me."

It happened so quickly, I didn't have time to react. The mischievous look on his face faded as his blue eyes turned red. Then he grabbed my face, and my breath lodged in my throat as he pressed his lips to mine.

I froze as his lips claimed mine, and I was pleasantly surprised at how warm they felt. My eyes fluttered closed as his hand tightened just a little on my face, and a moan rumbled in my throat. Goosebumps sprouted over my flesh as his hand slid around to my neck, holding me in place.

My lips parted the moment his tongue swiped against them. It was as if an explosion was going off inside me as his tongue began to explore my mouth. His other hand gripped my waist, and I found myself leaning into him as our kiss deepened. I'd wanted this. I'd wanted to feel him and taste him so badly.

Why, though? Why do I want him like this?

I pushed my fingers into his wet hair, and my heart lodged in my throat as he began to lower me onto the grass. My body felt weak and completely at his disposal as he towered over me. I wasn't thinking about how wrong this was—that I was a werewolf and he was a vampire. All I could focus on was the incredible way he made me feel.

His red eyes didn't scare me anymore as they darted back and forth over my face. He ran a knuckle down my cheek to my throat, and my body shuddered from the feeling of his skin on mine.

His fangs appeared, the tips peeking out from his slightly parted lips, as he used his thumb to trace my mouth. "Sweet Elinor," he whispered against my lips before kissing me gently. His cheek brushed against mine as the hand that was still holding my neck moved my head to the side, leaving my throat bare for him. "Are you scared?"

I closed my eyes tightly as I felt his fangs touch my skin. "No . . ." My reply was breathy, my voice almost unrecognizable to me. "I-I'm not afraid."

He leaned up to look at me once more. "It's not wise to give a vampire access to your neck like this, Elinor."

"Well, it's you. You won't bite without permission, right?" I asked as I reached up to touch his face.

Using his heightened speed, he quickly snatched my hand and kissed the tip of my middle finger. "No. I'd never hurt you," he said, his jaws clenched. "But I do want to taste you. I've wanted to taste you from the moment we met. But I can't." He released my hand. "I doubt I'd be able to stop."

I knew I should be afraid, very afraid. After all, he'd just told me he wanted to feed on me. But all I could think about was the way his words glided from his lips. He lowered his head to my throat, and a whimper escaped me as he kissed my flesh gently.

"You've never been touched before, have you?"

My cheeks began to warm, and I looked away with embarrassment. "Do you have to say it that way?"

He chuckled. "Tell me you want me to."

My eyes found him quickly. My heart hammered against my chest as I thought of the reason I'd come here. I'd planned to tell him goodbye. I didn't come for this. I was about to be married—I shouldn't be doing this!

"I have no intention of making this our last meeting, Elinor. I hope you know that." He released the back of my neck, and his hand made its way down my side to caress my thigh. "All you have to say is please."

I exhaled while shaking my head, trying to snap out of the daze I found myself in. "I can't. You know nothing can ever happen between us."

He lowered his face to mine as if to kiss me.

All of a sudden, a thundering voice yelled out from behind us, "What the hell do you think you're doing?"

I snapped out of my stupor as Connor's angry voice pierced the silence. I jumped up rapidly and found Will already on his feet.

I took a step forward, ready to explain myself, even though I had no clue how I'd make Connor understand why I was giving myself to a vampire. Realization of what had almost just happened hit me, and I placed my hand over my neck.

But I had no time to think about that, because Connor started to shift. The rage in his eyes terrified, and it only intensified when Will took my elbow. "Get away from her!" Connor yelled as he fell onto his hands and knees, his wolf breaking free to howl loudly.

My blood ran cold as the warning echoed through the forest. I knew within minutes, we'd be surrounded by more wolves. There would be nowhere for Will to run.

Goddess, what have I done?

THE BLOODMOON WARS
CONTINUES...

THE BLOODMOON WARS (A PARANORMAL
SHIFTER PREQUEL SERIES TO LUNA RISING)

The Enlightenment: Book 2 The Bloodmoon Wars (A Paranormal
Shifter Series Prequel to Luna Rising)

https://ssbks.com/BW2

Pissed and on the verge of ripping someone to shreds, I didn't think before I ran off into the forest during a full moon.

Not the SMARTEST move... I know.

So *of course*, I was attacked

by a thirsty ***vampire***

...only to be saved by another.

He wasn't like the **ghastly** creature that had tried to rip my throat out,

No, he was *DROP-DEAD GORGEOUS.*

That's how I met **Will Hunter**

...a vampire that's as mysterious as he is handsome.

Is it crazy that…

I kept going back to that spot every night to meet him?

Do you know what's crazier?

Being CAUGHT kissing him by my pack's beta.

My world is about to be flipped onto its head

...and there is nothing I can do to stop it.

https://ssbks.com/BW2

HAVE YOU READ THE FREE BLOODMOON WARS PREQUEL?

https://ssbks.com/BWPrequel

Either my whole village dies… or I make the ultimate sacrifice.

As the son of our village's shaman, I'm expected to marry a virgin bride. But I only have eyes for pregnant widow Ava, who is off-limits for me.

And because life isn't twisted enough, I get another curveball thrown at me...

Plagued by a dark vision, my father binds my soul to my body in an attempt to save me from the worst of what might await. But I'm not relying on a ritual to save myself--I'm going to find out what he saw... and stop it.

Soon I come to realize there's no way I'll get out of this mess alive.

When vampires attack our village, the vampire Queen offers me a terrible choice--one with implications for more than just the survival of Ava and the rest of my clan.

If I give into the Queen's demands, I'll spend an eternity of darkness at her side as the very thing I despise most. With everything and everyone I love at stake, I'd gladly give my life to save my village.

But can I condemn the rest of the world to the monster I'll become?

This is the prequel to the Bloodmoon Wars series.

Are you wondering how Will became a vampire? Click

below to get your FREE copy of the The Dark Ages (Bloodmoon Wars Prequel)

https://ssbks.com/BWPrequel

ALSO BY SARA SNOW

THE LUNA RISING UNIVERSE

THE BLOODMOON WARS (A PARANORMAL
SHIFTER SERIES PREQUEL TO LUNA RISING)

The Dark Ages (FREE Prequel)

https://ssbsks.com/BWPrequel

The Awakening (Book 1)

https://ssbks.com/BW1

The Enlightenment (Book 2)

https://ssbks.com/BW2

The Revolution (Book 3)

https://ssbks.com/BW3

The Renaissance (Book 4)

https://ssbks.com/BW4

The New Age (Book 5)

https://ssbks.com/BW5

LUNA RISING SERIES (A PARANORMAL SHIFTER
SERIES)

Luna Rising Prequel (Free Download)

https://ssbks.com/LunaPrequel

Luna Rising (Book 1)

https://ssbks.com/LR1

Luna Captured (Book 2)

https://ssbks.com/LR2

Luna Conflicted (Book 3)

https://ssbks.com/LR3

Luna Darkness (Book 4)

https://ssbks.com/LR4

Luna Chosen (Book 5)

https://ssbks.com/LR5

WOLF REBORN SERIES (A PARANORMAL SHIFTER SERIES) - NATALIE'S SERIES

Enchanted Reborn (Free Prequel)

https://ssbks.com/WRPrequel

Wolf Reborn (Book 1)

https://ssbks.com/WR1

Wolf Burdened (Book 2)

https://ssbks.com/WR2

Wolf Scorned (Book 3)

https://ssbks.com/WR3

Wolf Fallen (Book 4)

https://ssbks.com/WR4

Wolf Embraced (Book 5)

https://ssbks.com/WR5

THE VENANDI UNIVERSE

THE VENANDI CHRONICLES

Demon Marked (Book 1)

https://ssbks.com/VC1

Demon Kiss (Book 2)

https://ssbks.com/VC2

Demon Huntress (Book 3)

https://ssbks.com/VC3

Demon Desire (Book 4)

https://ssbks.com/VC4

Demon Eternal (Book 5)

https://ssbks.com/VC5

THE DESTINE UNIVERSE

DESTINE ACADEMY SERIES (A MAGICAL
ACADEMY SERIES)

Destine Academy Books 1-10 Boxed Set

https://ssbks.com/DA1-10

ENJOY THIS BOOK? I WOULD
LOVE TO HEAR FROM YOU...

Thank you very much for downloading my eBook. I hope you enjoyed reading it as much as I did writing it!

Reviews of my books are an incredibly valuable tool in my arsenal for getting attention. Unfortunately, as an independent author, I do not have the deep pockets of the Big City publishing firms. This means you will not see my book cover on the subway or in TV ads.

(Maybe one day!)

But I do have something much more powerful and effective than that, and it's something those publishers would kill to get their hands on:

A <u>WONDERFUL</u> bunch of readers who are committed and loyal!

Honest reviews of my books help get the attention of other readers like yourselves.

If you enjoyed this book, could you help me write even better books in the future? I will be eternally grateful if you could spend just two minutes leaving a review (it can be as short as you like):

Please use the link below to leave a quick review:

https://ssbks.com/BW1

I LOVE to hear from my fans, so *THANK YOU* for sharing your feedback with me!

Much Love,

~Sara

ABOUT THE AUTHOR

Sara Snow was born and raised in Texas, then transplanted to Washington, D.C. after high school. She was inspired to write a paranormal shifter series when she got her new puppy, a fierce yet lovable Yorkshire Terrier named Loki. When not eagerly working on her next book, Sara loves to geek out at Marvel movies, play games with her family and friends, and travel around the world. No matter where she is or what she is doing, she can rarely be found without a book in her hand.

Or Facebook:
Click Here
https://ssbks.com/fb
Join Sara Snow's Werewolf Council:
https://ssbks.com/fbgroup

www.ingramcontent.com/pod-product-compliance
Lightning Source LLC
Chambersburg PA
CBHW070449200726
48293CB00007B/2143